The Heart of the Woods
and Other Stories

———————

The Heart of the Woods
and Other Stories

Zoe Storm

Olympia, WA

The Heart of the Woods and Other Stories © 2026 by Zoe Storm

First Antithesis Press paperback edition, published 2026

Cover design by Laura Tempesta

Editing by Emma Canady, Kathryn Walton-Elliott

Design and Layout by Antithesis Press

This is a work of fiction. Unless otherwise indicated, all names, characters, businesses, places, events, and incidents in this book are either the product of the author's imagination or used in a fictitious manner. Any resemblance to actual locales, organizations, events, or actual persons, living or dead, is purely coincidental. This book contains no LLM / AI generated content.

All rights reserved. No part of this book may be reproduced or used for training artificial intelligence/large language models (or similar systems) in any manner whatsoever without written permission, with the exception of the use of brief quotations embodied in critical articles and reviews. For further information or to seek permission contact:

Antithesis Press, LLC.
120 State Ave NE #175
Olympia, WA 98501
United States of America

info@antithesispress.com
www.antithesispress.com

Antithesis Press logo © 2025 Antithesis Press

Logo designed by Delyth Williams

Library of Congress Control Number: 2026931424

ISBN: 978-1-969858-04-8

3 5 7 9 10 8 6 4 2

Contents

The Sacrifice	1
The Heart of the Woods	22
The Prophecy	38
The Princess and Her Hunter	55
A Christmas Gift	77
Afterword	105

Contents

The Sacrifice

THALIARD STOOD BEFORE me, staff at the ready. "Hold still for a moment, this will take but a second," he said. I dipped my head in acknowledgment. He raised his staff and gently tapped me on each shoulder. Quirking his mouth in concentration, he spoke carefully, "Ετ ξε ηυμαδ αυγησ ωβελεδ τε."

As I always did, I gritted my teeth as the wound in my arm knit together. Within a couple seconds, it was as good as new. "Ow," I complained.

"Oh, Jo, baby," Rowan said, leaning down to plant a kiss on top of my head.

"Don't worry, Ro," I replied with a smile. "It didn't hurt *that* bad, it was just a flesh wound. And that bandit got what was coming to him."

She smirked. "Damn right." She hefted her ax, which had a chip in the blade, the metal sporting a noticeable dark-colored hue, then she turned to Thaliard. "Okay, my turn."

The healer nodded. He tapped Rowan's shoulders, and repeated, "Ετ ξε ηυμαδ αυγησ ωβελεδ τε."

Rowan grimaced and hissed through her teeth as her wounds — much more numerous than mine, not to mention deeper — healed. It took much longer for my wife's skin to be whole and unmarred, but after Thaliard was done, even her ax looked to be newly forged.

"Damn," she said under her breath. "That bloody well hurt."

"What did you expect, for it to tickle?" Kian laughed. "Seriously, Rowan, we keep telling you that you don't need to put yourself at risk like that each and every time."

"If I don't do it, who will? At least this way the bad guys focus on me instead of y'all, so y'all have time to cast your spells and sling your arrows." Rowan punched Kian's shoulder. "Nice job on nailing that one guy trying to outflank me, by the way."

"My pleasure."

"But you could, maybe, take a couple steps back when I shout a warning?" I asked. "This way you won't get caught in the blast radius. I know you get your anti-magic wards refreshed every time we're in town—"

"Thanks for that, by the way," Rowan said, nodding at Thaliard, who signaled acknowledgment.

"—but my spells hurt. It's what they're designed for."

Rowan quirked her mouth. "They don't hurt *that* much."

"Because the bad guys take the brunt of them. What if I miss? What if I hit you instead?"

"I trust that you won't," she said, and she leaned over again to give me another kiss.

Kian smirked. "You two are so cute. You never kiss me like that," she called to Lysa, who was visible through the window, sitting outside the healer's house while she sharpened her longsword on a whetstone.

Lysa paused, looked up, and raised an eyebrow. "That's because you're not tiny and cute like Jo is."

"Hey!" Kian protested. "Am too!"

"Nope. You're beautiful, not cute, and you're definitely not tiny."

"Oh, come on," Rowan interjected, "Jo's not tiny, either. He's…" She paused, bit her lip for a moment, then concluded, "Compact."

Kian nodded. "Yeah, that's probably the best descriptor."

I pouted. "Y'all are a bunch of bullies."

"Excuse me," Thaliard said, and we all turned toward him. "Much as I'd like to stay here and watch you ladies…and gentleman," he added after a moment, "flirting with each other, I have some patients to visit, so if you don't mind…?"

He raised a hand, palm upwards. Rowan grabbed her purse and counted out three gold coins and two silver ones into Thaliard's hand. The healer nodded in turn, pocketed the gold, but handed the silvers back to Rowan.

"Fixing your equipment was a freebie," he said. "Pleasure doing business with you."

THE SACRIFICE 3

"And with you too," Rowan said. Kian, Lysa, and I nodded in agreement.

We made our way out of the house, Thaliard locking the door behind himself. "Do be careful out there. I like you folks, and I'd hate it if anything unfixable happened to you."

He put his hat on, tipped it to us, and walked off toward the center of town.

"Well then!" Rowan said, clapping her hands. "What do you say we turn the bandit scalps in at the guardhouse, then go grab a drink and something to eat at the Wooden Washtub? I, for one, am famished."

"As am I," Lysa said. "Fighting takes a lot out of you, especially if you're on the front lines."

Rowan nodded. "Let's go."

≡

"Cheers!" We chorused while knocking our tankards together.

"To another job well done," Kian added, and took a swig. "Man, the beer here is always wonderful."

"Bit too warm for my tastes," Rowan commented. She looked at me and wordlessly extended the tankard toward me.

I nodded and, waving my hand, I murmured "ᛟᚠᚨ," under my breath.

"Thanks, hon," Rowan said. She took a drink and smiled. "Much better," she added, placing the tankard down on the table next to her plate.

"You've gotten really good at that," Lysa said. "I remember the first time you tried it, Rowan had to wait for it to thaw before she could drink it."

"I hadn't learned how to really control my magic just yet," I replied. "It takes a bit to figure it out. Correct volume, intonation, hand gestures. Fine-tuning spells is hard, throwing them out at full power is much easier."

"Oh, speaking of which," Kian said, "did you see the bandit leader's face when his shield burst into flames? It was really funny."

"Hey, it's his fault for parrying my fire spell. And I held back. I didn't want to turn anyone into a charred corpse." I took a drink and then smirked. "We still needed to collect the scalps, after all."

Everyone at the table erupted into uproarious laughter. "See? My hubby is the best," Rowan said, reaching over and mussing my hair. "Still don't know what I did to score a man like this."

"No, I don't know what I did to make you fall in love," I rebutted.

"Yeah, what *did* you do?" said a new voice. "Honestly, I don't think you deserve Rowan."

I grimaced. I took a moment to compose myself before turning around and saying, "Hi, Shelton, what's up?"

"That's *Mister* Shelton to you, squirt," the huge man said, scowling down at me; then he looked up at the girls seated around the table, grinned roguishly, and said, "Hello, *ladies*."

"Hi, Shelt," Rowan said, ice in her voice. "Haven't seen you in a while. I'm surprised you're still alive, I thought you'd died like a leek-bug somewhere."

"I'm alive and well, thank you. What about you? Still hanging out with this puppy, I see."

"I'm still *married* to this puppy, Shelton. Very happily, I should add."

Shelton scoffed. "Whatever. Look me up when you decide you're tired of scraps and want to see what being with a real man is like."

He turned on his heel and started to walk away. As he did so, I flicked a finger in his direction and whispered, "ᛟᚠᛇᚱ."

Shelton put his foot down and slipped on the hair-thin layer of ice that had formed under the sole of his boot; he fell heavily to the floor, grunting in pain.

"Interesting. So real men are those who trip on their feet while walking on a perfectly flat floor. Guess I should take notes," I commented snidely.

"Why, you…" Shelton growled, planting a hand on the floor and pushing himself up, drawing his sword from his belt.

In an instant, Rowan and Lysa were on their feet and brandishing their weapons, while Kian rolled back off the bench, grabbing a knife from the table as she did so, and I knew she could turn it into a projectile as deadly as her arrows if she needed to. I, for my part, sat perfectly motionless. The tavern's common room was perfectly still, too, and deathly silent; all eyes were on us.

"You wanna go, Shelton? By all means," I said, glaring a challenge up at him. "But you're alone, while there's four of us. Not to mention a roomful of witnesses who will gladly tell the guards you were the first to draw steel."

Shelton returned my glare and, for a moment, I was afraid he would still try to attack me despite the clear disadvantage he was at. He thought better of it, shook his head, and sheathed his sword.

"What*ever*," he said. "You're not worth the bother anyway. I've got better things to do. See you."

He turned around again, and that time I let him walk away. Lysa, Kian, and Rowan relaxed, put their weapons away, and sat back down at the table. The background noise of the tavern quickly resumed.

"Bloody hell," Lysa said under her breath. "I seriously thought that fucker was going to go for it."

"As did I," I said. "We could've taken him, no doubt, but probably not without having to make another trip to Thaliard's afterwards."

"Yeah. Honestly, Jo, you really shouldn't have riled him up like that," Kian said.

"What, you're blaming him?" Rowan said, frowning.

"Not at all. That idiot slipping was very funny, and he deserved it, and he'd have deserved the beating we would've given him if he hadn't backed down. But sometimes it's best to pick your battles."

I dipped my head. "Yeah, sorry about that. My bad. But I couldn't resist." Kian smiled. After a moment, I turned to Rowan. "And, speaking of battles, what should we do tomorrow? Do we have anything lined up?"

"I talked with the captain while I was waiting for the clerk to count out payment for the scalps," she said. "They're assembling a team to go clear out that pack of direwolves who've been harassing travelers on the forest road, and he asked if we wanted to take part in it. Pay's pretty good, even taking into account that we're going to have to split it with the other parties."

"Oh?" Lysa said, raising an eyebrow. "It wouldn't be just us?"

"No," Rowan shook her head. "Too many wolves for just one party, and there's rumors of a pair of fell wolves leading the pack. They want at least a dozen people for this job." She looked around the table. "Wanna go for it? It will be more dangerous than our usual fare, but it shouldn't be a problem."

"Yeah, sure," Kian said.

Lysa nodded. "Been a while since I had wolf meat."

"Oh? Is it tasty?"

"Good in a stew." She frowned. "You've never had it? We've been dating for what, two years? I thought I'd have made some for you by now."

"You didn't."

"I'll do it this time then."

"Speaking of food," Rowan interjected, and pointed at the plates full of meat and veggies and bread. "Shall we eat? That idiot got me worked up, and I'm famished."

"Yeah, of course," Lysa said. She grabbed some meat off her plate, put it in her mouth, chewed, and scowled. "Damn, it's already cold."

"Allow me," I laughed. I waved my hand and muttered, "ᚠᛦXᛦ."

≡

"ᚠᛦXᛦ!" I shouted, stabbing my finger toward the direwolf. The fire spell hit it in the head, singing its fur, and it turned toward me, snarling. As it did so, Kian shot three arrows in quick succession, all of which pierced the beast in the side. It shuddered, took a step toward me, staggered, then finally collapsed to the ground. "Thanks, Kian," I said.

"Any time, Jo," she replied.

"Hey! Little help here?" Lysa's voice called from my left, somewhere in the forest undergrowth.

Kian looked at me, and I nodded. "Go," I said. "I'll go look for Rowan and the others."

She nodded back and rushed off in the direction Lysa's voice had come from. I turned around and ran in the opposite direction, toward where I'd seen Rowan heading a few minutes earlier.

It wasn't supposed to go like this. It was supposed to be a normal job. A bit more difficult than usual, sure, but the guards had been very thorough in recruiting capable people, and in the end nearly twenty people had ventured into the forest to fight the direwolves.

And were promptly ambushed by them.

The attack had come without warning. One moment we were making our way through the brush, the next four people on the flanks of our column had been grabbed and dragged off, their screams of fear quickly turning into ones of pain before cutting off entirely. It had only been thanks to Rowan and the captain of the guard, who'd rallied the rest to form a defensive circle, that we hadn't been completely overcome right away. We'd managed to fight off the first wave of beasts that had come our way without losses before killing one of the two fell wolves, a terrifying beast nearly as tall as Rowan, who'd come charging at us with a half-dozen direwolves behind it.

Then a few overeager people had decided to go chasing after the stragglers. The captain had ordered everyone to follow them to avoid splitting up the team, but the group had nonetheless become separated very quickly in the thick, shadowy forest, and I'd ended up with Kian and a swordsman whose name I didn't know facing two direwolves. We'd managed to kill both of the beasts, but the swordsman had lost his life.

I shook my head as I rushed through the undergrowth. When we got back to town there would surely be several complaints about how this mission had been handled, but I didn't have time to worry about that right at this moment. First I had to make sure my wife was okay, and then find a way to make sure as many people as possible got out of the forest with life and limb intact.

Hearing a noise to my right, I planted my feet and skidded to a stop. I cautiously ventured through a few bushes and found myself at the edge of a clearing. In the middle of it, Rowan, injured but still on her feet, was standing tall, shifting her position every now and then to keep herself between her foes — the remaining fell wolf and a pair of direwolves — and the two other people who were with her: the guard captain, sprawled on the forest floor, either dead or out cold, and Shelton, who was kneeling, a hand clasped firmly on his sword arm to stem the blood flowing from a wound. Rowan wasn't wielding her ax, I noticed, but a longsword instead, likely the captain's. Her weapon of choice was several feet away from her, embedded in a direwolf corpse, which was crumpled in a heap along with two others. I smiled; she'd clearly been busy.

But now she needed my help because, as I watched, the fell wolf and the direwolves exchanged a glance, seemingly of understanding, then one of the two direwolves started circling around the clearing, clearly hoping to catch my wife in a pincer move. I hadn't been noticed yet, and I realized this was a good opportunity. I concentrated on my magic, pushing as much of it as I could up to my hands, then thrust my arms forward, both palms toward the lone direwolf, and shouted, "ᛊᚹᚱᚠᛊᛗᛁᚱ!"

The detonation spell hit the beast dead center in the middle of its body, which split cleanly: the front and back, including the head and tail, fell to the forest floor a couple feet away, while the middle section all but disintegrated in a shower of meaty, bloody fragments.

The fell wolf and the remaining direwolf flinched, and I took the chance to rush out of the undergrowth and into the clearing, taking position by my wife's side. She grinned. "Glad to see you're still in one piece, Jo," she said. "How's the situation?"

"Kian was alright when I left her, and I think Lysa is alright, too," I replied. "I don't know about the others. And I don't know how many wolves are left, but not that many, probably."

She nodded. "Alright. Let's get rid of these two and try to regroup with the others. Shelton, how's your arm?" she called over her shoulder. "We could really use an extra hand over here." A pause. I heard a branch snap. "Shelton?"

I glanced behind me just in time to see the man scrambling away from us — and away from the wolves — and into the forest while screaming and dropping his sword in the process.

"Oh, that bloody *coward*," Rowan bit out. "Alright, guess it's just the two of us."

I nodded grimly. This wasn't going to be easy, especially since the two remaining wolves had split up once more and were circling us, again trying to catch us from both sides. "I'll take the big one," I said.

"But—"

"No objections. You're injured, I'm the one who's got the best chance against it. You take the small one."

THE SACRIFICE

"Alright. It won't get past me, guaranteed."

I kept shifting my position. By now the wolves were on opposite sides from us, and I was standing almost back-to-back with Rowan. I licked my lips in concentration and focused my magic in my hands. "Okay, let's see how the big guy likes this. ᚠᛈᛁᚱᛁᛊᛁᛏᛁᚱ!"

The fell wolf had seen the attack coming and stepped to the side as I let loose the spell. It flew well clear of the beast and obliterated a tree behind it. "Alright, how about this then? ᚠᛊᚷᛊ! ᚠᛊᚷᛊ!"

The two fire spells, thrown out in quick succession, hit the giant wolf in the side, but when the smoke had cleared a couple seconds later it looked no worse for the wear. As a magical beast, it probably had some degree of resistance, akin to the anti-magic wards Thaliard regularly placed on Rowan.

I grimaced; there was no way I was going to be able to take it down with basic spells, I realized, but everything else I had was too slow. The fell wolf would easily dodge any spells that took more than a fraction of a moment to cast.

The beast kept circling, keeping its eyes locked with mine. Behind me I heard some noise, but I didn't dare glance over my shoulder to see how Rowan was faring against the direwolf.

"ᛋᛁᛊ!" I shouted, slashing my arm, but the ice spell bounced harmlessly against the fell wolf's fur in a burst of glittering crystals.

Still useless — there was no way I could manage to hit it where it hurt. Unless I got closer, that is, close enough so it wouldn't have time to dodge a detonation spell. But that would be very dangerous, as it would bring me within striking range of the monster's teeth and claws, and—

I inhaled sharply. A thought had just shot through my head. There was, in fact, a way I could manage to hit the fell wolf. It was a terrible idea, to be completely honest — if I mis-timed it by just a couple seconds, I would end up dead, and then the fell wolf, with the direwolf's help, would make quick work of my wife.

And that was what did it. The thought of Rowan dead, her body savaged by the beasts, was enough to spur me into action. I stepped forward, letting loose two more ice spells followed by a fire one. Then I took another step, and as I did so I pretended to trip, letting myself fall down on one knee. The fell wolf let out a grunt of surprise, but it was just a brief moment — it was smart enough not to let a chance like that slip by, and it rushed toward me, opening its jaws.

I gritted my teeth as the beast bit down on my shoulder, its fangs sinking into my chest and back, and let out a scream of pain. "Jo!" I heard Rowan shout behind me, but I paid her no mind — I was too focused on what I had to do.

I raised my arms and placed a hand on each side of the fell wolf's enormous head. "Gotcha, ya mutt," I said, and pushed all my remaining magic power into my palms.

The monster realized what I was about to do and opened its mouth, let me go, tried to draw back, but it was too late. With a shout of "ᚅᛈᚱᚠᛖᛗᚱ!" I let loose the strongest detonation spell I'd ever cast in my entire life.

The blast threw me clear of the beast, all the way across the clearing. I smashed into a tree and felt a few bones break before falling to the forest floor. The pain was almost unbearable, but I willed myself not to pass out; I gritted my teeth, planted a foot, and pushed myself back up to a standing position. I looked over at where I'd been standing just a few moments earlier — the fell wolf's headless corpse was slumped in the middle of the clearing, and next to it, Rowan was getting back on her feet. The direwolf was nowhere to be seen; it had likely fled.

Behind Rowan, at the other end of the clearing, Kian, Lysa, and a couple other people burst through the brush. "Jo! Rowan!" Kian shouted. "Are you alright?"

"Hey, guys," I said. "Glad you could join us. How did you find us?"

"We followed the noise of fighting, and—" Lysa began. Then she gasped in shock and put a hand to her mouth.

"Jo..." Kian said, her eyes wide.

"What?" I asked.

"Jo, your...your arms!" Rowan said.

"What about my arms?" I said, then I looked down, and I realized I couldn't see my hands — I didn't *have* hands, in fact, my arms ending in two stumps just above where the elbows should've been. "Oh."

"Jo!" Rowan shouted, rushing across the clearing to me as I fell down on one knee. "Jo!"

"Guess I really messed up this time, didn't I?" I murmured. Now that the shock and the excitement of the battle had left me, it was getting hard to stay awake. "But at least you're okay, Ro." I gave her a weak smile.

"Jo!" She shouted again, grabbing me and cautiously lowering me to the forest floor. "Jo, stay with me!"

"Someone call a healer!" Someone — probably Kian — shouted.

"Jo!" Rowan called again, but I couldn't hold on any longer.

"I love you, Ro," I whispered. I closed my eyes and fell asleep.

≡

"Do *something!* You can't just let him *die!*"

"You don't understand, Rowan. He's lost too much blood. His body is too damaged. There's no way a simple healing spell…Hm."

"What was that? Did you have an idea?"

"I…may have something. There's one thing I can try. But if I mess up, it may kill him outright."

"I trust that you won't mess up. And besides, we've nothing left to lose, Thal."

"It will be extremely painful, the shock alone may kill him."

"But he *will* die if you don't do it, right?"

"Yes."

"Let's do it, then. Kian, Lysa, give me a hand here. Jo? Sweetie? I'm here. Wake up, please."

"Uhn…Ro?"

"Yes, it's me. Stay with me a moment longer, please. Thaliard? Do it."

"Alright. Here goes. Εαυτ εαμηνα ηραλπμεξε βα μαυτητσερ μαμρωφ μανητσηρπ νη μυυτ συπρωκ."

I felt a searing pain course through me. I screamed. And I passed out again.

≡

I was woken up by the noise of a door opening and closing. "Mmm…" I murmured, stirring a bit.

"Oh, sorry, didn't mean to wake you up," Thaliard said. I opened one eye and found myself looking up at him, smiling kindly at me. "But you've been sleeping for quite a while in any case, so it's about time you opened your eyes. How do you feel?"

"I feel fine," I said. "What happened? Where am I?"

"My house. My bed, to be precise, but I don't mind, you needed it more than I did. What's the last thing you remember?"

I scrunched my forehead in thought. "I remember...the fell wolf. And casting the spell. And..."

I blinked; I raised my left arm and looked at my hand, turning it, flexing my fingers.

Thaliard chuckled. "Yes, we did fix that. And the other one."

I nodded, tried to raise my right arm, too, but found that I couldn't. Looking down I saw that my hand was being held firmly in place by Rowan gripping it tightly. She was sprawled in a chair beside the bed, bent over, head resting on the mattress, sleeping soundly.

"She didn't leave your side even for a moment," Thaliard said with a smile. "You're a very lucky...um...person."

"Person?" I said, frowning.

Thaliard just looked at me for a moment, then shook his head. "Alright, hold on a second." He marched across the room and opened the door. "Hey, Jo's awake. Can you come in here? Bring the mirror and some chairs."

"Right!" A voice — which I recognized as Kian's — replied.

Thaliard nodded and walked back to the bed and, upon reaching it, he poked Rowan in the shoulder. "Wake up. Come on, wake up."

Rowan stirred. She unconsciously gripped my hand a bit more firmly before her eyes fluttered open. She blinked, then smiled. "Jo! You're awake! You're okay! You *are* okay, right?"

"I am," I reassured her. "Thank you, Ro. You bringing me here saved my life."

She shook her head. "No, you coming to my rescue saved *my* life. And you killing the fell wolf probably saved *everyone's* lives. You're a hero, Jo." She smiled a wry smile. "Though you were more than a bit reckless. You almost died."

I smiled at her. "I'd gladly do it again for you."

"Please don't," she replied, shaking her head again. "You gave me such a scare. To see my...To see you like that..."

I frowned. "Why the hesitation?" I asked. "What's happening?"

"We'll tell you in just a moment," Thaliard said as Kian and Lysa joined him and Rowan around the bed. They all sat down, looking at me.

"Still can't believe it," Kian said, shaking her head.

"Still can't believe what?" I said.

"I..." Rowan began. Hesitating, she bit her lip. "I'm not quite sure how to say it."

"I'll do it," Thaliard said, and Rowan nodded. "Alright. Jo, when you were brought here, you were very close to death."

"Yeah, that part I figured," I replied. "After what I did..."

Thaliard nodded. "Just a couple hours more, just a *few minutes* more, and you probably wouldn't have made it. You were lucky I was home, and I could take care of you right away. But you were in such bad shape that my usual spells didn't have any effect on you. So, to save you, I had to do a full regeneration."

"And what does that mean?"

"It's a spell I only use in the direst situations. The details are very technical, but the spell basically separated your body and your soul, then completely destroyed your body and rebuilt it from scratch based on your soul's pattern. You can easily understand how such a thing can go wrong. If I'd messed it up, your soul could've been lost, and you would've been dead."

"But you didn't mess it up, since I'm here."

"No, I didn't mess it up. But the spell had some...unforeseen consequences."

I frowned. "Such as?"

"Like I said, your body is reformed according to the pattern of your soul. And your soul, apparently, had a pre-existing condition."

"Pre-existing condition?"

"Well...Let's see, how do I—"

"Okay, let's stop beating around the bush here," Rowan said. "Kian?"

Kian nodded and handed Rowan a mirror, which she placed in front of me. I blinked at my reflection. Since the last time I'd seen myself, my face had apparently become much softer. My hair was also longer, and my beard was nowhere to be found. In fact, the person I was looking at looked like—

"Wait, I'm a girl?!" I exclaimed.

"A woman," Lysa said. "Girls are young. You're what, twenty-eight?"

"Twenty-nine," Rowan rebutted. "And twenty-nine is young."

"Is not."

"Is too," Kian said, slapping Lysa's shoulder. "Just because you're twenty-five it doesn't mean that anyone older than you is automatically old."

"Says who?"

"Says—"

"I think we're getting sidetracked here, this is entirely beside the point," Thaliard interjected. "But yes, Jo, you're a girl, a woman, female, however you want to put it."

Lysa nodded. "An innie instead of an outie, two bumps instead of flat, sits to pee instead of standing..."

"*Lysa*," Rowan said, glaring at her.

"Sorry."

"But..." I began. Everyone turned to look at me.

"But...?" Kian prompted.

"But you can fix this, right? I mean, you can turn me back into a man?"

Thaliard shook his head. "No, I'm sorry, I can't do that."

"Why not?"

"Because there's no spell for that. And please don't yell at me," he continued when he saw me open my mouth, "Rowan has already done that, at length. It's a wonder she didn't lose her voice."

I glanced at my wife, who smiled and shrugged sheepishly.

"But what about the Tiresians?" I asked. "Don't they change their sex?"

Rowan frowned, as did Kian. They exchanged a look. "What's a Tiresian?" Kian asked.

"People who are born of one sex, but identify with the other," Lysa replied. "That would be women who were born as men, and men who were born as women."

"There's people like that?"

"Oh yes," Lysa nodded. She was looking at me, a smirk on her lips. "How do you know about the Tiresians, Jo?"

"How do *you* know about them?" I rebutted.

"My sister's one of them," she replied. "What about you?"

"I…" I paused. I shook my head and turned back to Thaliard. "Anyway, what about the Tiresians?"

"Well," he replied, and he stroked his beard. "I have, on occasion, used the full regeneration spell to help Tiresians, but first, that's always very dangerous. And second, that wouldn't help you anyway."

"Why not?"

"Because, as you'll remember, the spell reconstructs your body based on your soul's pattern. And that pattern doesn't change, ever. So even if I used the spell on you, the result would be the same."

"Oh. So, I'm stuck like this?"

He nodded. "I'm afraid so, yes."

I bit my lip, taking a moment to digest the thought; then I shrugged. "Okay."

My friends all blinked at me. "Okay?" Rowan said. "You mean, you're okay with this?"

"Kinda, yeah?" I replied. "I mean, it doesn't feel that different from before. I feel fine, actually. I probably would go back to being a man if I could, but since I can't, yeah. This is fine." I paused, realizing something. "Wait, what about you, Ro?"

"What *about* me?" she asked.

"Are you fine with me being, well…" I gestured down at myself, then continued, "I mean, you like men, don't you? Do you…" I bit my lip again. "Do you want to split up? Get a—"

"No!" She quickly said, and she grabbed my hand and gave it a squeeze. "No, not at all, Jo. I mean, besides the fact that I don't like *just* men—"

"Wait, what?" Kian said.

"Yeah, did I never tell you?"

"No, you didn't."

"Huh. Weird, I thought I did. Anyway, besides that," she continued, looking back down at me, "I didn't marry you for your looks."

I blinked. "Hey!" I exclaimed. "What's that supposed to mean?!"

"I mean that what you look like — what you *looked* like — was a very distant second compared to what made me choose you among all the other people I've ever met."

"And that would be...?"

"That you're kind and caring and brave and an excellent person besides," she said, and I felt my face go red. "I doubt any of that has changed now that you're a girl—"

"A woman," Lysa said under her breath. Kian punched her.

"—so yes, you're still the person I want to share my life with."

I looked at Rowan, at my wife, for a few moments, then I couldn't hold out any longer. I sprung up from the bed, threw my arms around her neck, and pulled her down with me as I fell back to the mattress, drawing her into a deep kiss at the same time.

It lasted a while. At some point one of our friends — Lysa, probably — wolf-whistled at us.

"Thank you, Ro," I said, once we'd come up for air.

"No, thank you, Jo," she replied, smiling at me. "For being you."

"Well!" Kian exclaimed. "This calls for a celebration!"

I gave her an askance look. "A celebration?"

"Yeah! You're still alive and still together, so we have to celebrate that. And besides, we still haven't had a proper victory feast after we came back from the mission since we were so worried about you. So, what do you say we go over to the Wooden Washtub and drink something?"

"Yes, I think I could go for a drink," I said.

"Just the one," Thaliard said. "She's still in recovery, don't let her drink too much."

"We won't, don't worry," Kian replied. "Lysa, do you mind going on ahead and grabbing us a table? We'll be right along."

"Of course," Lysa said. She stood up from her chair and, after saying "See you later," she walked out of the room.

I looked at Kian curiously. "Why aren't we going with her right now?"

"That's because while Lysa arranges for everything, me and your wife are going to find you something to wear."

"I have something to wear. I have my clothes."

"Yes, but since this is your first time out on the town as a girl, you should dress up a bit. Wear something nice," Rowan said.

"Like a dress," Kian said.

"Like a dress," Rowan nodded.

I looked from one to the other and back again: they were sporting identical, impish smiles. I sighed.

≡

"Yo! We're here!" Rowan said, waving at Lysa, who was standing just outside the Wooden Washtub, waiting for us.

"Took you long enough," Lysa replied, then she looked me up and down. "You look nice."

I looked down at myself for what was probably the millionth time. I'd borrowed a dress from Kian — which I'd seen her wear before. On her it fell to just above her knee, while on me it was longer, coming down to my mid-calf — and wearing it felt weird, but also good, somewhat liberating. And, after looking at myself in the mirror, I had to agree that I *did* look nice. "Thank you," I said. Lysa nodded and smiled at me.

"Hope you didn't wait too long," Kian said.

"Little bit, but at least this way I had enough time to arrange for everything," Lysa replied.

"Everything?" I asked.

"Oh yes. Right this way, ma'am." She opened the door and walked inside the tavern, pulling me by the hand, while Rowan and Kian pushed me. "Here she is, folks!" she called out at the top of her lungs. "The woman of the hour!"

As soon as I stepped over the threshold I was greeted by a loud cheer. Everyone had stood up from their tables and was shouting and whooping and whistling and clapping their hands.

I looked around, bewildered. "What's this?" I said as I was pulled to the middle of the room.

"It's a celebration for you, of course," Kian said, grabbing a tankard from a table and placing it in my unresisting hands.

Rowan nodded. "I wasn't kidding when I said that you saved all of us by killing that beast, Jo," she said. "And apparently everyone agrees so they wanted to thank you. They've been waiting to throw this party ever since we told them you'd made it through Thaliard's treatment and would survive."

"Though they didn't tell us anything about you becoming such a lovely lady until just now," the guard captain said, stepping up in front of me. He held out his hand. "On behalf of the entire town, I thank you for everything you've done."

I hesitantly took his hand and shook it. "Oh, it was nothing, really, anyone would've done the same."

He shook his head. "Hardly. Some people, in fact—"

"Hey, hey!" said a voice. "What's all this, then? A feast? And I wasn't invited?"

The room fell silent. We all turned to look at Shelton, who'd just walked through the front door. He was making his way through the crowd, looking around.

Rowan, Kian, and Lysa exchanged glances. "We didn't think you would come," Lysa said flatly.

"Why wouldn't I come? I never miss a celebration," Shelton said. Then his eyes fell on me. "Say, who's the new gal?"

Rowan hesitated. "Uh…" she said.

"Well well well! Hello, ma'am!" Shelton said, ambling toward me. "I must say, you look very fine. Do you come here often?"

I blinked. He hadn't recognized me? I did, admittedly, look quite different from how I'd looked the last time we'd seen each other — and apparently, he was the one person in town who hadn't been told about my change. So, I should probably rectify the situation right away, right?

…Or on the other hand…

"I don't, actually," I said, putting as much sweetness in my voice as I could. "In fact, it's my first time here. I was visiting a friend," I motioned toward Rowan, "and she said this is a nice place, where you can meet lots of interesting people, so here I am. Right, Ro?"

Rowan boggled at me, as did everyone in the room. Shelton didn't seem to notice, however.

"*Right, Ro?*" I repeated.

"Uh…Yes," she said, shaking herself out of her daze. "I thought she might like it, since it's a celebration. The whole town is here. A good chance to make some friends."

THE SACRIFICE

"Good, good," Shelton said. "What's the celebration for, anyway?"

"Something about wolves?" I half-said, half-asked.

"Oh, yes! We've recently managed to exterminate some nasty beasts which were threatening merchants on the forest road," Shelton replied. Then he leaned in and stage-whispered, "Even though, truth be told, I was the one who did all the work."

"Wh—" Kian began.

"Oh really!" I exclaimed, cutting my friend off, shushing her with a quick motion of my hand just outside Shelton's view — it wasn't hard, his eyes were focused on my face and my breasts. "You must be a very good hunter, then."

"That I am," Shelton replied. "And a good fighter. The best hunter and fighter in town."

"I should've guessed." I sidled up to him and ran a finger over his arm. "After all, you're *very* handsome. And you look like you have an excellent…" I cupped his crotch with my hand, "*Weapon.*"

"Oh, you should see what I can do with my weapon."

"Mhm. What did you say your name was again?"

"Shelton."

"Can I tell you something, Shelton?"

"Yes, of course."

I gripped his crotch a bit more firmly, raised myself on my tip-toes, leaned in, and whispered into his ear, "ᛟᚨᚱ."

I stepped back as Shelton screamed and doubled over, his hands moving to his crotch. "Fuck!" he shouted, then fell down to his knee. "Fuck, that's cold!"

"Oh, come on, it's just a little frostbite," I said. "It can't be worse than a direwolf's bite, can it?"

"What the fuck did you do that for, you cunt?!"

"Hey!" Rowan exclaimed. "Watch what you call my wife!"

Shelton blinked. "Your wife…?" he said, looking at her. Then he looked at me again. "Jo?!"

I smiled sweetly at him. "Hi, Shelton," I said.

His face went red. "Why, you…" he said, and he started to get to his feet.

"Watch it, man," the guard captain said, placing a hand on his shoulder. "Don't start anything you can't finish."

"Oh, I'll finish it alright!"

"Like you finished the fell wolf? By running away?" I said. "Everyone knows you're a coward, Shelton. That's why you weren't invited tonight."

A murmur of agreement ran through the room, and many people nodded as Shelton looked around.

"But tell you what," I continued, drawing his attention back to me. "I'll take you on any time. A formal duel. Just say when and where."

Shelton frowned. "Bitch," he spat out.

"I may be a bitch, but I have more balls than you. You should get yours looked at by a healer, by the way."

Shelton's frown deepened as mocking laughter rang out. He unsteadily got to his feet, looked around, scowled at me, then took a step toward the door, saying, "This isn't over."

"Oh yes, it is," the captain said. "You're a good fighter, Shelton, so I put up with your shit until now. But you ran away from a fight, leaving your allies behind. And what's more, now you come here and insult the woman who stood her ground and saved my life, and more lives besides? Yeah, no, you're done." He shook his head. "I want you out of town before dusk tomorrow. And see that you don't come back."

Shelton blinked at him, then he looked around, but was only met with stern, scowling faces. "I don't need to wait until dusk tomorrow," he said. "I'm leaving now. And fuck the lot of you." He turned on his heel and walked out of the tavern.

I let out a breath. Out of the corner of my eye I saw Lysa drop her hand from the hilt of her sword, and I nodded my thanks to her.

"Do you think we'll see him again?" Kian asked.

"Don't know, don't care," I replied. "What I care about now is celebrating." I spun around to take in the room and grabbed a tankard, raising it high. "Cheers!" I called out.

"Cheers!" everyone chorused, and the noise of merriment started filling the tavern again.

Rowan stepped up to me. "Well, I must say, it looks like my wife is kind of a natural at being a woman. Nice act you put up there."

"Why, thank you," I replied. I rose on the balls of my feet. She leaned down, and we kissed. "You know," I continued after we'd separated, "I thought it would be awkward to be a woman after being a man all my life, but you know what? It's fine. This is fine."

"Glad to hear that," my wife said, and she kissed me again.

The Heart of the Woods

THE PHONE'S ALARM clock goes off at six thirty on the dot. As always, it starts playing a happy, cheery song, one Aileen really liked once upon a time but has since come to hate with the fiery passion of a thousand suns. She turns over in bed, slams her hand a couple times into the night stand, then gropes around, grabs the offending device, moves it up to her face, and fumbles with it for a bit — seriously, why did she ever think installing an alarm clock app that forces you to do math first thing in the morning was a good idea? — before it finally goes quiet.

"Good morning, Aileen!" The phone's assistant says cheerfully. "The time is now half past six. Right now, the temperature is sixty degrees Fahrenheit, and the weather is overcast. The forecast for today is cloudy, with isolated showers, and a maximum temperature of eighty degrees. Have a nice day!"

Aileen groans. She always hates how happy Mr. Phone seems to be when waking her up from a nice sleep. "Good morning and fuck you too, buddy," she murmurs.

And then frowns.

She experimentally clears her throat a few times: deep, rough, rasping. *Do I have a cold?* Aileen thinks, and moves her hand up to touch her neck, which only makes her frown deepen — what's an Adam's apple doing there? She experimentally gropes around it. As she does so, the back of her hand brushes along the underside of her jaw, and she feels stubble.

Her eyes shoot open. Her cellphone drops from her grasp, bounces once on the bed, and thuds down to the floor, but she pays it no mind: she's too busy using her hands to explore her body, frantically moving them around, feeling her face, her chest, her—

She sits bolt upright in bed and swings her legs off, jumping up and running to the wardrobe. She throws the door open, looks in the mirror, and a face she hasn't seen in a year stares back at her. A male face.

"No," she whispers. "No no no no no..."

She pinches the back of her hand, then slaps her own face as hard as she dares, feeling the pain. It's not a dream.

"No," she says again. "No..."

"Mmm..." Ava murmurs, stirring in bed behind her. "Aileen?" she asks, pulling herself partially up. "What is— Who are you? What are you doing here? Where's Aileen?" she demands, a tinge of panic in her voice.

Aileen gulps, pushes down a wave of distress which threatens to overwhelm her mind and senses and make it impossible for her to function, and turns around, looking at Ava directly. "It's me, Ava," she answers.

Ava blinks and looks at her. Then, after a moment, comprehension dawns on her face. "Oh," she says. She pauses briefly before she continues, "So you've turned back."

Aileen sighs deeply. "Yeah," she says, shoulders slumping. "I...I'm sorry, Ava."

"Hey now, no," Ava says, pushing the covers aside and standing up. "None of that talk, Aileen." She hesitates. "Is it still...?"

"Aileen is fine. For now."

A nod. "Aileen. I promised you I would stand by you, stand *with* you, even if you turned back. I'm not going to go back on my word."

She reaches out and hesitantly touches Aileen's hand; Aileen flinches and steps away. "Sorry," she says. "I'm sorry. It's just...I don't want to be touched right now."

Ava looks at her for a moment then nods again. "Alright. No touching until you say so." She pauses. "I'll go make some pancakes for breakfast. Just...take your time."

She grabs her robe off a hanger and walks out of the room and to the kitchen, leaving Aileen alone with her feelings and her thoughts. And one thought in particular keeps coming back to her, over and over again: *Why? Why now? Why after all this time? It's not fair.*

The pancakes are cold by the time Aileen emerges from the bedroom and makes her way to the kitchen. She's changed out of her cute pink PJs and into an old tracksuit she usually only wears on laundry day when she has nothing else left. It's the last piece of male clothing she owns. She sits down heavily at the table, across from Ava.

"Hi," Ava says with a smile, pouring coffee for Aileen and then for herself. Aileen grunts in response. Silence hangs between them while they eat.

"So, how are you feeling?"

Aileen looks up at her from the remains of her breakfast. "Fine."

Ava's eyebrow rises. "Just fine? Huh. I mean, it's okay if you're *fine*, your feelings are your own, I'm not going to tell you how you should feel," she replies. "But you know...I thought you'd be happy."

Aileen's eyebrows knit together briefly. "Happy?" She asks.

"Yes. Happy." Ava nods. "I mean, we met just after...*that* happened, right? And for a few weeks, maybe two months, you kept saying that you wanted to go back, that you hoped you would change back as soon as possible. You stopped talking about it after a while, true, but as I recall the last time we talked about it you said something along the lines of, 'Since there's apparently no way back, I might as well get used to it.' You seemed really reluctant."

Aileen gulps. "Yeah. Yeah. I mean...If I think about it, I'm happy. I guess."

Ava looks at her girlfriend for a moment. Then she takes a deep breath, as if to prepare herself. "I'm sorry, but you don't seem very happy to me."

Aileen looks blankly back at her. "Why wouldn't I be happy? After all, I finally changed back into a man. This is what I wanted all along. So, yes, I'm happy," she concludes, her voice flat and emotionless.

"Okay," Ava says carefully. "So, I guess I can go back to calling you—"

"No!" Aileen interrupts sharply. "No. Aileen is fine. After all, it's the name we picked together, isn't it? The one I had before doesn't..." She gulps. "Doesn't feel like *me*. I'll have to pick another one eventually. But for now, Aileen is okay."

Ava nods again. "Okay," she repeats. "So, what do you want to do today? As I recall, we were planning on meeting with The Gang, but if you don't want to..."

Aileen considers Ava's proposal. The Gang is the affectionate nickname for their friend group, and that day they were going to meet for lunch and spend the afternoon shopping. It was something Aileen's looked forward to all week, but she really doesn't feel like going right at that moment. On the other hand, maybe getting some fresh air and seeing her friends will cheer her up? And shopping, too — after her change, shopping had quickly become one of her favorite pastimes.

But there's a hitch. She looks down at herself, and frowns.

Ava senses her girlfriend's hesitation. "I'm going to send a message in our group chat, tell them we can't make it today," she says. Then, after a moment's pause, she continues, "Do you want to go out at all? Just the two of us, no one else."

"...Yeah, I'd like that. To take my mind off...this. Thank you, Ava," Aileen says.

"You're welcome," Ava replies, and reaches across the table to take Aileen's hand — but yet again, Aileen flinches back. "Alright," Ava says, raising her hands in surrender. "I'll go get changed, and I'll send that text."

She stands up from the table and walks to the bedroom as Aileen mentally kicks herself. *Stupid. Stupid, stupid, stupid. She's trying to help you*, she thinks. *Just let her.*

But then again, is it Aileen's fault that she hates it when someone touches her body?

It's just as it had been before the change had happened. One year to the day after she'd walked out of the forest she's back in her original body, and she's immediately backsliding.

What even the hell? This is what she'd wanted all along. *All along.* Even though she never really thinks about it that much these days — these months, actually — Aileen is sure she should be happy at being male again. Why isn't she?

She gets up from the chair and walks to the living room bookcase. It takes her a moment to spot the folder. Pulling it out from between two books, she opens it.

'MISSING HIKER COMES BACK AS A WOMAN!' the title of the newspaper clipping proclaims. Aileen rolls her eyes at that — always with the dramatics, you'd think she'd gotten it from a tabloid instead of the newspaper of record: the quality of their writing had been really slipping — and starts reading.

'A hiker who had been missing for a week after getting lost in Ramsey Forest has been found safe and seemingly in good health; however, authorities and doctors alike are stumped, as the hiker has allegedly changed sex. Mr. ▇▇▇ Walton—' Aileen smiles at the blacked-out word. She'd scratched it out when, on her first re-read of the article after signing the deed poll, she found out she was frowning every time she came across a mention of her former first name '—has been able to conclusively prove his identity, but investigation is on-going as to what exactly has caused such a radical change in his body. Mr. Walton has been unable to provide any insight, since he says he has no memory of his week-long ordeal.'

And that had been the truth. Aileen had woken up curled under a tree, confused and female, and had wandered through the woods for half a day before being found by the search party. Proving she was who she said she was had been surprisingly easy, but thinking about it after the fact, it made sense. She simply had too much knowledge of her life up to that point (personal and family history down to the tiniest detail, full and complete knowledge of medical information, bank account numbers, and the precise location and contents of her brother's hidden porn stash) for anyone to be able to deny her identity. Not to mention that her fingerprints and DNA both matched what she'd left behind — except for the Y chromosome, of course.

A battery of medical tests had followed, one after the other, which had conclusively proven she was fully female. 'And, ah, fully functioning,' as one of the doctors had oh so helpfully put it. They'd wanted to investigate further, but Aileen had balked at the huge number of procedures they wanted her to undergo (more and more invasive as she ran down the list), so after a week — and after taking out a restraining order on the journalists who kept following her wherever she went — she'd simply decided to go on living her life, and to forget all about her sudden change. She met Ava a couple weeks later as she was trying to figure out how women's clothing sizes worked: Ava saw Aileen needed help and offered it, they hit it off, and that was that.

"Ready," Ava says, walking into the living room and shaking Aileen out of her thoughts. "I've warned The Gang, so they know we're not coming today. I haven't told them about…" She gestures at Aileen, and Aileen nods. "So, we can go once you change."

Aileen looks down at herself, at her horrible, ratty tracksuit, and frowns. "I have nothing to wear," she says. "This is the only thing that fits me. The current me, I mean. Everything else is too small or the wrong shape."

Ava smiles kindly in return. "Guess our first stop will be a clothes store, then," she says. "We'll grab a few things."

"Not too many," Aileen replies. When Ava raises an eyebrow, she continues, "I mean, I could change back tomorrow, right? Then our purchases would be wasted."

"Right," Ava nods. "Okay. Let's go."

≣

Unlike the previous times she'd been in a foul mood before going out with her girlfriend, being out and about, chatting with Ava, and especially going shopping does nothing to cheer Aileen up. It's as if the whole world has taken on a black tint, a darkness that overshadows even the overcast sky and makes it impossible for her to be happy.

The shopping trip is particularly miserable. She finds herself looking at dresses and skirts and tops and jackets and shoes, none of which she'll be able to wear ever again. Even if she somehow manages to find the right size — a nigh-impossible prospect, given her new body shape and measurements — everyone will just look at her as if she were a cross-dressing man.

She's so depressed she almost forgets she has to grab some male clothing, so she can have something to wear besides a tracksuit, but when she remembers she wastes no time in selecting a pair of jeans, a T-shirt, and a hoodie. Wearing those, weirdly, is somewhat comforting, since it brings back memories of her life before the change, when a jeans-and-hoodie combo was what she wore in all but the most formal of occasions.

She's so out of it she barely notices Ava steering her toward their favorite cafe, the one that makes the best waffles in town, and whose owner, Chloe, is tirelessly friendly and cheerful. Clearly Ava thinks having brunch, one of Aileen's favorite activities, will lift her spirits a bit, and Aileen finds herself agreeing with Ava as she glances at the menu in the window — there are some topping combinations in there she's wanted to try for a while, and there's no time like the present.

Chloe smiles at Ava as they walk into the cafe, but Aileen is met with a slight frown of non-recognition, which she can't help but notice. As usual, Chloe gives them some time to choose before she comes by with a smile and a notepad. Always the one with weird tastes, Ava picks tomato waffles with basil ice cream.

"Alright, got that," Chloe says brightly, and then she turns to Aileen. "And what would you like, sir?"

If you asked Aileen how she got home that day, she wouldn't be able to answer. She's pretty sure Ava must've helped her, but that's a deduction made after the fact, since she can't remember anything between Chloe asking her for her order and coming to hours later, lying on the bed, face buried in a pillow soaked with tears, Ava whispering soothing words into her ear while rubbing her back.

The first words Aileen says after coming out of her trance are simple: "I have to go back."

Ava just sighs in response. "I'm really sorry, Aileen, but how? After all, you have no idea what caused your change, in either direction. How can you go back to being a woman?"

"I wasn't talking about that," Aileen says, shaking her head. "I know I can't just snap my fingers and turn back, no matter how much I want to. I have to *go* back."

"Go back where?" Ava asks.

"To where this all began. Ramsey Forest." Aileen takes a deep breath, and continues, "It was there I changed the first time. And maybe there, I will find an answer."

"Okay. How can I help?"

THE HEART OF THE WOODS

≡

As it turns out, the help Ava can provide is gathering equipment and supplies. It takes a day to get everything together, since about six months after her change, Aileen had given away her old hiking clothing and boots and bought new ones, which of course don't fit her anymore, so they have to buy them anew. Aileen's backpack, however, is still the one she had a year before, as is most of her equipment, which is old and well-loved — it had been her father's before his arthritis had taken a turn for the worse and he'd passed everything on to her.

So the next day — a day she spent being miserable since, even by busying herself, she can't forget the sheer *wrongness* that radiates from her body — Aileen stands at the edge of Ramsey Forest, in the exact same spot she had a year before, looking deep into the foreboding woods.

"Are you sure you don't want me to come with you?" Ava asks.

"I'm sure," Aileen replies. "I don't know how or why, but there's this nagging feeling in the back of my mind, which keeps telling me I have to do this on my own."

Ava nods. "Okay. Be careful, though."

"I will. I'll come back to you, Ava. I promise."

"You better," Ava says with a smile.

They exchange a brief hug — very brief, since Aileen still very much dislikes being touched — and then she turns around and walks into the woods.

≡

Ramsey Forest is deep, dense, dark, and ancient, some of the trees near the edge being over four hundred years old, and there are probably even older ones deeper in. It had been one of the first areas in the country to be designated as a national park, but even before then, people seldom ventured inside. It's rumored to be haunted, and the souls which have walked in and never walked out over the centuries number in the hundreds.

There are some trails cut through the woods, mostly near the edge, so that hikers can explore the forest safely, but that isn't where Aileen is headed. Instead, she turns off the beaten path very soon, and keeps walking, moving deeper and deeper between trees and bushes, making her way through the undergrowth. It's slow going, but she's an experienced hiker and, after stopping for the night twice, she finds herself in the heart of the woods. It was there she'd woken up a year before, after her change and there, maybe, she will find her answer.

The light is fading as Aileen makes camp for the third time. She builds a small fire and places a small pot of water over it to heat up as she unrolls her sleeping bag...and then stops.

She thinks she's seen something out of the corner of her eye. Something that looks almost like mist, moving through the trees. But when she turns to look at it directly, she finds that she can't — the shape seems to move, always keeping just barely out of her sight. And maybe she's going crazy, but she thinks she can hear something too, just barely louder than the quiet crackling of the firewood. Something that sounds vaguely like someone breathing...or like a whisper.

"Is someone there?" She calls out. "Show yourself, please."

When the answer comes it is not through words, but through a feeling. Through emotions, which Aileen feels deep inside her heart: cheerfulness, happiness, elation at the fact that she's come back, and that maybe she can provide Them with the answer.

Aileen frowns. "The answer? What answer do You want me to give You?"

There is puzzlement now: she doesn't remember? How come? But then chiding, as if someone is reprimanding a child, telling them that *of course* she doesn't remember, They've done things specifically that way.

"I'm sorry, I still don't understand," Aileen says, her frown deepening. "What exactly have You done this way?"

Hesitation. Concern. A brief discussion. Finally, a decision: They will show her.

Aileen barely has time to blink when a tall misty figure comes into view and touches her in the center of her forehead with a long finger. She feels Their touch reach deep inside her mind, down into the most hidden recesses of her soul, until They find a knot which They had left there a year before, and untangle it.

And Aileen remembers.

≡

███ sits down heavily on the forest floor and leans back against the tree. This is it. By his estimation, this is the deepest one can get into Ramsey Forest, the deepest someone can walk in before starting to walk out. It has taken him over two days to reach that point, hiking alone, as ███ always does. He has no one to hike with, after all, no one he is really close to.

He doesn't even bother taking off his backpack. It's better this way, after all — when they find him, they will assume that he suddenly felt sick while hiking, sat down for a moment to catch his breath, and never got up again. The autopsy will likely be inconclusive. Several weeks deep in the forest, exposed to the elements, will make sure of that. In the end, the coroner will probably write down 'natural causes' and leave it at that.

Time to do it, then.

███ reaches down and unhooks the flask from his hip. He uncaps it, gives the contents a tentative sniff, and grimaces. He's always hated the taste and smell of alcohol, and the fact that the flask, besides vodka, also contains every last kind of benzo and antidepressant and tranquilizer he had in his medicine closet at home — everything his psychiatrist has had him try, unsuccessfully, to get rid of his depression — is sure to make the concoction taste even more awful. It's almost a shame it will be the last thing he will ever taste.

Almost.

"Farewell, then," ███ muses, and he raises the flask to his lips...and then stops.

He thinks he's seen something out of the corner of his eye. Something that looks almost like mist, moving through the trees. But when he turns to look at it directly, he finds that he can't — the shape seems to move, always keeping just barely out of his sight. And maybe he's going crazy, but he thinks he can hear something too, just barely louder than the quiet thumping of his heart in his chest. Something that sounds vaguely like someone's breathing...Or like a whisper.

"Is someone there?" he calls out loud. "Show yourself, please."

When the answer comes it is not through words, but through a feeling. Through emotions, which ▮ feels deep inside his heart: a greeting. Happiness at meeting someone after so long. Puzzlement at why he doesn't seem startled, or afraid — after all, it's not every day one comes across the In-Between — the place where worlds meet, where emotions rule and shape reality — and encounters someone from Beyond.

▮ laughs. "It's been a while since I last felt anything, friend. Not even fear."

The mood is now questioning: They thought humans *did* feel emotions, and very strongly, too. Why does he not?

"Dunno," he says, waving with his flask. "It's been like this since I was twelve or thirteen. Everything is just...dull. Flat. My psych tells me it's depression, but he has no idea what causes the depression itself."

There is interest now. A discussion, of which ▮ can only grasp the vague outline, but which seems to involve him. Then They have another question: while They never had much contact with humans, They had been under the impression that emotions, especially happiness, were what made life worth living. Then, how is ▮ still alive?

"You don't mince words, do You?" ▮ replies. "Well, as it turns out, You're right. I'm not alive. Not really. I'm just...coasting through life. Like a zombie, just shambling forward. That's a kind of walking corpse," he adds, reacting to a shift in the mood. "So I've decided to just stop. To just lie down and stop moving for good. That's why I came here."

The emotions are startled now; even if ▮ spoke cryptically, They understood what he meant. Is he really going to end his life?

"Yup," he nods in response. Then he realizes something. "I guess this will leave quite a mess here on Your doorstep, won't it? Well, sorry about that. But thank You for the conversation."

He raises the flask to his lips once again.

Alarm. Wait! Stop!

"Why should I?"

THE HEART OF THE WOODS

He isn't quite sure he can interpret the way the mood shifts, but They seem to think that it would be a waste. If he's going to throw away his life, why not give it to Them?

"What for?" He asks, honestly puzzled.

Excitement now. It seems that They have thought of an experiment of sorts. They will figure out why he doesn't feel emotions, by looking deep inside him, and fix that.

"You can do that?!" ▆▆▆ exclaims. "You can…just fix me?"

They can. But — and the emotions shift, swirling, the discussion becoming more and more animated — there is a problem. If ▆▆▆ knows They have changed him, it will contaminate the experiment. Invalidate the data. So They have to make him forget all of this. But then, an objection: if ▆▆▆ forgets and walks out of the woods, how will They know the result of the experiment? After all, They cannot set foot on Earth — They cannot leave the In-Between.

"I promise I'll come back," he says. "In a year. I will come back and tell You how my life has been. If Your experiment has been successful."

Impossible. Either he knows what happens, which would invalidate the experiment, or he will forget and won't come back.

▆▆▆ tilts his head and considers Their dilemma. "Well then, there must be *something* You can do," he says. "Some way to make sure I will seek You out again."

The mood becomes very still for a moment as They consider his words. Yes. There *is* something They can do.

"Well then, do it. I have nothing to lose."

▆▆▆ barely has time to blink when a tall misty figure comes into view and touches him in the center of his forehead with a long finger. He feels Their touch reach deep inside his mind, down into the most hidden recesses of his soul, until They find what They are looking for: the reason he cannot feel emotions. So They eliminate that reason, They change him, and They tie his memories into a knot.

And ▆▆▆ forgets.

Aileen gasps as her eyes shoot open, and she finds herself staring at a vision that is almost heavenly, almost angelic. Instead of the misty creature which had stood in front of her, the humanoid is fully formed, and Their presence is bathing her in a white radiance.

"You...look different," she says in a shuddering voice, her mind still reeling from the violation that has just occurred.

Amusement: of course They look different. After all, they are in the In-Between, where emotions rule and shape reality. They have no fixed form themselves, instead taking on a shape determined by those They meet. Right at that moment, Aileen is grateful, and Their form matches how she feels.

Aileen nods. "Yes. Yes, I do feel grateful," she says. "It was thanks to You that I finally figured out why I just felt numb. That I figured out who I really am."

Of course. They know that, They know the answer to Their question, having pried it from the depths of her mind.

"I...I'm not sure I really like that," Aileen frowns. Was she wrong about Them? Suddenly, Their radiance seems to diminish.

They pay no heed to her words: They are too elated at the results of Their experiment — They had no idea that a mismatch between soul and body, unbeknownst even to the person themselves, could cause someone such significant distress. Gender! What a concept! They will have to think long and hard about this.

Aileen smiles. It's weirdly amusing to see such an otherworldly being so excited. But still, there's something she has to ask Them. "Okay, so now You know. Then can You change me back?" she says.

Puzzlement. Change her back? Why?

"Well, because...Because I helped You out?" she asks, her eyebrows knitting together. The light coming from Them diminishes further. "So I thought You would help me out in turn."

Amusement now. Hilarity, almost. Why would They do that? After all, They have obtained the results They had sought. What Aileen does with her life from this point on is no concern of Theirs.

Aileen's frown deepens, and she stares at Them. They're radiating no more light now. Instead, They seem almost dark — no longer soft and comforting, They're angular and menacing.

"I'm sorry, but I hardly think this is fair," Aileen says. "You showed me how my life could be, and now You're snatching it away from me? Just like that?"

This time the mood is plain, matter-of-fact, and can be read as clear as writing on a page: yes. Just like that. Why? Does Aileen have any objections? And if so, what is she going to do about it?

Aileen is puzzled for a moment, surprised at the emotions she's feeling. She always thought that someone telling her They can help her, but won't, would make her feel sad. That it would make her feel depressed. That it would make her feel hopeless.

But, bizarrely, she doesn't feel sad, depressed, or hopeless.

Instead, Aileen is *angry*.

"Listen now, You..." she says, stepping forward and making a grab for Them. Her hand touches nothing but air, even though she was sure she reached far enough.

Amusement. Seriously, what does she think she's doing?

She glares, the emotions coming from Them only fanning her rage. "I don't know what I'm doing. I have no idea who You are, or what this place even is, but I can promise You one thing." She steps forward and reaches out again, and this time her hand grabs something — it's almost like grasping a knot of wood, tangled roots in what is now a horrible eldritch being, and she *pulls*, bringing herself close to Them. "If You don't change me back right now, I *will* find a way to make You pay somehow."

They are mildly surprised now. No one has been able to touch Them in centuries. But they are also still amused. Somehow, she said? They have been here, in the In-Between, for millennia. They have met many humans who have called Them by many names — Aesir, Fae, elves, spriggan, goblins, and more — and promises such as the one she just spoke have been often made, but never kept.

Aileen grips her hand tighter, feeling splinters dig into her fingers and palm, and reaches with her other hand, redoubling the grasp she has on Them. She moves closer still, face-to-face, and it's like staring into an abyss. "Then I will be the first one to keep it," she swears, her eyes and soul filled with determination.

And then she realizes something: besides Them, the forest around her is also changing, turning dark and twisted to match her mood, branches bending down, leaves like arrowheads, bearing down on her and Them both. Aileen is momentarily startled, and the branches retreat for a moment, but then She realizes what is happening, and focuses all of Her sadness, all of Her anger, and all of Her sorrow, makes them into a weapon, forges them into a blade. The woods which surround Her change to match, the trees sharpening even more, otherworldly flames swirling between the trunks.

Now They are concerned. Alarmed. They tell Her to stop. Doesn't She realize what She's doing? Her emotions are causing an imbalance in the forest around Her. If She keeps going, the In-Between will soon collapse, it will cease to exist, and everything inside it will cease to exist too!

Aileen grins, licking Her lips, tasting Their emotions. "Good," She says. "That will teach you a lesson."

They have no mouth to scream with, but what they are feeling is incredibly clear: She must stop! If this keeps going, She will die too! And She doesn't want to die, does She?!

She drinks all of their feelings in and savors them: their alarm, their panic, and one emotion in particular they have clearly never felt before — deep, unbridled fear. "What, have you forgotten?" She says, Her voice mocking. "Ancient as you are, I thought you'd remember what happened a year ago, but you clearly don't. Because if you did, you'd remember what I said to you back then: *I have nothing to lose.*"

The sharp trees — branches like claws, leaves like blades — keep closing in on them, as does the darkness, as do the flames. Aileen keeps pushing, relishing in their despair while feeling oblivion overtake Her, and She's about to sink fully into the abyss when She feels them relent: They will do it! If She stops, they will change Her back! But She has to stop! She must stop, before it's too late!

"Say please."

Please!

Everything stops.

It's as if time has frozen around them, the otherworldly weapons fixed in place, moments away from piercing human and eldritch flesh alike. Aileen smiles and releases Her grip.

"Good choice, buddy," She says, reaching up and lightly slapping their cheek. "It was a pleasure doing business with you."

She steps back and steadies Herself. "Do it."

They reach up and touch Her forehead, and the In-Between disappears from Her sight, the universe dissolving into light.

※

Aileen is momentarily confused when she wakes up. She looks around, eyes unfocused.

But then she remembers.

She gulps. Takes a deep breath. Reaches with her hands and feels her body and face.

She smiles.

"Thank you," she says aloud.

No one answers, but she thinks she can hear a concerned rustling of leaves up in the tree canopy.

Aileen gets up, dusts herself off, breaks camp, gathers her things, and walks away, without looking back. She has somewhere to be, after all. She's promised Ava she would come back, and she has a hell of a story to tell her.

The Prophecy

Gus took one look at the door, then turned to his wife. "Are you *really* sure about this, honey?" he asked. "After all, this is...um." He gestured at the ornate wooden plaque set beside the entrance, upon which the words 'Madame Alma Rasputin, Mistress of the Occult, Medium, Seer, and Channeler' were inscribed in complex and looping golden letters.

"What do you mean?" Terry said.

"I mean that this doesn't really inspire confidence."

Terry huffed. "Come on, Gus. Don't you want to help Dani?"

"Yes, but—"

Terry cut him off. "And haven't we tried everything else before resorting to this?"

"Yes, but—"

"I mean, we've been to psychologists, psychiatrists, counselors, even a *priest*," she spat out that word with clear distaste, "but no one managed to find out what is wrong with her. So, why not try this?"

"Because..." Gus said and stopped, clearly expecting Terry to talk over him again.

There was a moment of awkward silence.

"Because...?" Terry prompted.

Gus looked at her for a moment, then shook his head. "Because I don't believe in the occult."

Terry huffed again. "Well, *I* don't believe in god, but that didn't stop your mother from dragging us in front of that...that *man*. Ugh." She shuddered. "The whole time we were there, I felt as if I was being judged."

"Come on, dear, that's not true at all. He just said something about your hair, that's all," Gus soothed her.

THE PROPHECY

"What's wrong with having blue hair?" Terry retorted. "And, if you'll remember, he dared to suggest that my 'lifestyle choices' are somehow to blame for what Dani is going through. Seriously. The slap I gave him was more than justified." She flexed her hand and smiled at the memory.

"He couldn't have known you're bi."

"I'm pretty certain your mom told him, actually. Coming out to your parents was probably the biggest mistake I ever made," Terry said. "Anyway, shall we go in?"

Gus held her gaze for a few moments and sighed. "I guess there's no way I can talk you out of this, is there?"

"Nope!" Terry replied brightly.

"Okay then," Gus said and turned toward the door. On a quick inspection there was no doorbell visible, so he reached up to knock, but before he could do so, the door swung open.

"Please, do come in," a woman's voice said.

Gus and Terry exchanged a glance and then stepped over the threshold. A tall, raven-haired woman was waiting for them just inside, dressed in a flowing robe of blues and purples.

"Welcome, Augustus. Welcome, Teresa. The spirits have foretold your arrival." She paused before smiling. "And by 'spirits' I mean that you've made an appointment on my website. I do not use my gift for such trivial matters. Please, close the door."

"Or else the spirits will get out?" Gus said.

"No, not at all," the woman answered, not hearing — or choosing to ignore — the slightly mocking tone in Gus's voice. "It's just that this house is old, and the drafts are just *terrible*." She paused while Terry closed the door, and then continued, "I am Madame Alma Rasputin. A pleasure."

"Rasputin, huh. Any relation?"

"But of course," Madame Alma said, with another mild smile. "Want to see a picture of my great-great-great-grandfather? He had muscles to spare, and his eyes seemed to burn from the inside."

Gus looked at her in puzzlement, but Terry laughed. "Okay, that was a good one," she said. "I like you, Madame."

"Wait, what?" Gus asked, looking between Terry and Alma. "What was that about?"

Terry looked at him in puzzlement. "The lover of the Russian Queen? Ring any bells?"

"No?"

"What kind of music does your husband listen to?" Alma asked.

"Christian Rock, mostly," Terry replied.

"It was what I grew up with," Gus said. "My parents are very religious, you see."

"Behold!" Alma exclaimed, throwing her arms up. "The spirits are whispering something to me! 'This man should listen to better music,' I think they're saying." Both she and Terry laughed, while Gus frowned, shook his head, and grumbled something under his breath.

"Madame Alma, we're here to ask you something," Terry said. "You see, it concerns—"

Alma held up her hand. "Please, say no more," she said. "I prefer not to be aware of the reason my clients came to me before I consult the spirits. That would form a preconception in my mind which would affect the channeling."

Terry nodded. "Yes, I see."

"Please follow me," Alma continued. She turned around, sweeping her robe in a wide arc, and stepped through a set of double doors which opened on their own in front of her.

"I appreciate the theatrics, at least," Gus mumbled as he and Terry followed Alma, "but automatic doors have been a thing for decades."

Terry elbowed him in the ribs.

Madame Alma guided them down a corridor and through another set of double doors, which also opened on their own, and then closed again once Gus and Terry had passed. Behind the doors was a wide, open chamber, with tall windows which allowed the afternoon light to flood the room. The furnishing was sparse: only a few dressers along the wall, and a small, circular table in the middle, surrounded by several ornate chairs, upon which an embroidered cloth which was clearly covering a spherical object sat.

"Is that your crystal ball?" Gus asked, pointing at it.

Alma inclined her head. "It is. The Orb of Knowledge." She marched to the table and dramatically flung the cloth off the sphere, which was about a foot in diameter, almost clear with the barest hint of sapphire tint. It was resting on top of a circular lip, which rose about half an inch off the table. "I always cover it when I'm not using it."

A smirk tugged at the corner of Gus's lips. "Because you don't want to let the spirits see what you're doing?"

"What? No," Alma replied. "It's because crystal spheres are very good lenses. If the sunlight hits it just right — or just *wrong*, depending on how you see it — it could burn my house down."

"Huh," Gus said. "Didn't know that. And I didn't expect you to be so…candid."

"What do you mean?"

"Well, I expected more mystery, more…*mumbo-jumbo*, if you get what I mean."

Alma smiled. "We'll get to that, don't worry. It's just that, even though I often commune with the spirits, it doesn't mean they influence everything I do. Now give me just a moment here." She grabbed a chair and started dragging it away from the table. "Should've really gotten things ready before you folks arrived, but I got distracted. I apologize."

She pushed the chair against the far wall and then grabbed another one and another one, lining them up alongside each other, until just three chairs were left around the table.

"Okay." She nodded in satisfaction and turned to smile at Gus and Terry. "Please take a seat. We'll begin right away."

The three of them sat down around the table. Alma looked at the couple. She lifted her hands and clapped them thrice, the loud noise resounding throughout the chamber.

Suddenly the heavy curtains which hung by the windows slid shut, plunging the room into darkness. Terry gasped. Gus, on his part, mumbled, "Neat trick," but his voice was a bit unsure.

"No tricks, I assure you," Alma replied. "Just the spirits."

She placed her hands beside the crystal sphere, one on each side and spoke again in a low voice: "Spirits of the Earth, Wind, and Fire, rulers of Summer and Lightning and of the Blue Sky, I beseech ye: come hither, shine, and grant these two lost souls your knowledge."

Slowly but steadily, the Orb of Knowledge started shining. Just a little bit at first, but then it brightened up, until it was illuminating the trio in a soft azure glow.

"Wow," Terry whispered.

"'Wow' nothing, dear. It's a trick," Gus said. "There's a lightbulb or an LED or something inside the ball, or under the table, and that's what's making it light up."

Madame Alma looked directly at him and then abruptly grabbed the Orb and lifted it off the table. It didn't stop glowing. "Feel it," she said. Gus hesitated for a moment, but soon he reached out and ran his hand over the surface. It was perfectly smooth and unbroken. And when he looked at the table, he was surprised to see that it, too, had no openings visible in it.

And why did the room feel so cold? It had been quite warm when they'd come in, probably because of the light coming from the windows. What was going on? He looked down and saw that there was a mist, just barely visible in the low light, floating about a foot off the ground, lapping at their calves. He reached down to touch it...

"Can we move on before the spirits get annoyed and leave?" Alma asked, piercing Gus with a glare and making him jump. Gus gulped and nodded. "Good." She set down the sphere on the table once again, placed her hands beside it, and cleared her throat. "As I was saying. O spirits, give us a signal that you're willing to answer our questions."

The crystal ball flared brighter for a couple seconds, then dimmed. Alma nodded.

"Augustus, Teresa, place your hands upon the Orb of Knowledge."

The couple complied, pressing their palms against the sides. Alma placed her own hand on top of the sphere.

"Now think about the question you want the spirits to answer," she said and closed her eyes. Gus and Terry quickly imitated her, and their faces screwed up in concentration. "Hmm," Alma mumbled. "I see. Yes, I think I'm receiving a message. You are here to ask...about your daughter, Danielle."

Gus's eyes flew open as he gave a start of surprise. "How did you—"

"Your hand, please," Alma said, opening her eyes, and Gus noticed that he'd accidentally pulled his hand a fraction of an inch back from the crystal sphere. "It has to be touching the Orb or else I will get no reading."

"No." He shook his head. "Not until you explain how..."

"Gus. Please," Terry said, placing her free hand on Gus's arm. "Give her a chance."

Gus looked at her for a moment, then he nodded, and placed his hand upon the surface of the sphere again.

Alma nodded. "Good. Now, I see that Danielle...Danielle hasn't been doing well in school," she whispered. "She used to be an honors student, but recently, ever since she moved up to high school, most of her tests have been coming back marked as C or D or even worse."

Terry bobbed her head, mesmerized. "We wanted to—"

"You wanted to know what is troubling her, and how you can help her," Alma spoke over her. "And the spirits...Hm." Her demeanor turned somber. "The spirits are telling me Danielle is being bullied. Someone is targeting her, and it's causing her trouble. She is having problems concentrating on her schoolwork. And—"

"Someone has been *bullying my daughter?*" Gus roared, rising to his feet, his eyes burning with righteous rage. "Tell me who it is!"

"Your hand, *please*," Alma said. After a moment, which Terry spent tugging on Gus's arm, he sat back down and, grumbling under his breath, touched the Orb once more. "I cannot tell you who it is," Alma continued. "I do not know. The spirits are showing me Danielle through her connection to you, as you are here right now, but they cannot show me her own connections unless she is also present. I'm sorry."

She paused. Terry stared at Alma, wide-eyed, while Gus was all but glaring.

"Shall we continue?" Alma asked and waited until they both nodded. "I feel...I feel longing. *Pining.* Danielle...Danielle has feelings for someone. Someone who is very close to her. A friend, I think, though I cannot see anything clearer." She frowned. "I feel doubt. Danielle does not know how that friend feels about her, and that doubt is keeping her distracted."

Gus hummed. "Must be Annie," he mused. "I've seen how Dani looks at her whenever she comes over to study."

"No, wait," Terry said. "Are you saying Dani's a lesbian?"

"Well, yeah? Of course she is," Gus replied. "She told me as much last year."

Terry's mouth fell open in surprise. "She *told* you?"

"She did. I *do* talk with my daughter, you know," Gus replied, with some reproach. "We spent a lot of time discussing it, and LGBT issues in general." Then he frowned. "Wait — didn't she tell you?"

Terry looked at him for a moment, stunned, and then shook her head and answered, "No, she didn't tell me."

"Um. Crap," Gus said, his frown deepening. He looked down at the table and mumbled, "Guess I just accidentally outed her, then."

Terry placed her hand on Gus's arm again. "Don't worry, I won't tell her. And I'll pretend to be surprised when she *does* tell me, eventually." She paused. "But you're okay with it? I mean, your parents…"

"My parents are old-fashioned. Probably *too* old-fashioned." Gus smiled. "And I'm okay with you being bi, aren't I?"

"Guess that's true," Terry said, smiling back.

"May we continue?" Alma asked, and when Terry and Gus turned to her, they saw she was smiling, too.

Terry nodded. "Yes, please. Go on."

Alma nodded back. "I feel…that Danielle is worried about her fitness. Because of the bullying, and because of schoolwork, she has not been running nearly as often as she used to, and she is afraid it is taking a toll on her."

"Yes, she did mention that," Terry said. "Well, not the reason, but the fact that she was…slacking off, as she put it. Guess it wasn't slacking off."

"And I feel…I feel…" Alma said. "I feel nothing more. That is all that is troubling your daughter Danielle."

Gus nodded carefully. "Alright, so what do we do? How do we help her?"

Alma shook her head. "That, I do not know. The spirits cannot help with that. But if I may suggest something, it is to speak with your daughter. To make her feel your presence. To let you know you're there for her. When I was young and I was having trouble much like Danielle seems to be, my mother sat next to me one day and said, 'You don't have to tell me anything, but I will listen if you do,' and that is a precious memory I carry with me to this day." She smiled. "So, maybe try that?"

"We will."

"But she'll be okay, right?" Gus asked. "Dani will be fine in the end, won't she?"

Alma looked at him for a moment. "Do you want me to try a scrying? Free of charge. I don't usually do this, but I like you folks."

Gus and Terry exchanged a glance. "Yes, please. Do that," Gus replied.

"Alright." Alma nodded. She closed her eyes and started mumbling in a language neither Terry nor Gus could understand.

Suddenly, the Orb flared brightly, and Alma went rigid. Her eyes shot open, and she stared at the ceiling. "It is a few years from now," she said, in a voice that sounded almost otherworldly. "Danielle is graduating from high school. Full honors. She is smiling and happy as she takes her graduation picture, her mothers standing proudly behind her." She slumped in the chair. "That is what I have seen. I thank you, spirits, for your assistance, and for passing on your secret messages."

She clapped her hands thrice, and the Orb of Knowledge darkened. The curtains slid open all at the same time, bathing the room in warm sunlight.

Terry blinked rapidly and then squeezed her eyes, to help them adapt to the light — but at the same time she frowned. "Wait, what was that?" She asked. "Mothers? Plural? What do you mean?"

"I do not know," Alma said. "It's what I've seen, but I don't know what it means."

"Well, if you've *seen* it, then shouldn't you also be able to *describe* it?"

Alma shook her head. "No, I'm sorry. I say 'seen' as a way of making my clients understand, but it is more of a…" She paused and shook her head again. "In a scrying, the details are always indistinct. I saw a girl posing for a photo, and I *knew* it was Danielle, and I saw two women standing behind her, and I *knew* they were Danielle's mothers, but I could not describe any of them, not even Danielle."

Terry was still frowning. "Well, that's just silly," she said. "It doesn't make any sense. After all, I'm the only mother Danielle has; no one else can claim that title." She hesitated. "Except maybe if I were married to a woman? But that doesn't make any sense either, I'm married to Gus, and I've no intention of divorcing him and remarrying." She turned to look at her husband. "What do you think about this, Gus?"

Gus hadn't said anything since the Orb had turned dark. He was staring straight ahead, a shocked expression in his eyes, his mouth hanging open and his face pale as death itself, almost ashen: he looked like he'd seen a ghost.

"Gus?" Terry repeated. "What's wrong?"

Again, Gus didn't say anything, his mouth opening and closing seemingly on its own. He was completely out of it.

"Augustus, are you alright?" Alma said.

When Gus, yet again, didn't say anything, Terry turned to Alma. "What's wrong, Madame Alma? Has he been affected by the spirits somehow?"

Alma shook her head. "No, that's... Well, I won't say *impossible*, when the occult is involved, anything could happen. But I've done hundreds of rituals, and the spirits have never affected anyone but myself, and even that was only to pass on messages or show me visions."

"This *is* impossible," Gus said.

Terry turned back to him. "What was that? Dear, are you okay?"

"It's impossible," Gus repeated, and he leveled a finger at Alma. "*This* is impossible. The ritual has gone wrong somehow. Your vision was wrong. Do another scrying."

"I cannot do that," Alma replied, and she pointed at the Orb of Knowledge. "The spirits have left already. It will be at least a day until I'm able to call them forth again. They get grumpy if I bother them too much."

"Do another scrying, I said!" Gus shouted, rising to his feet. "And change your story! What you saw..." He stopped talking and screwed his eyes shut. Then to the immense surprise of both Terry and Alma, he sobbed. "What you saw was *wrong*. It cannot be right." He sobbed again. "It just *can't*."

"Gus, holy cow, what?" Terry asked, staring at Gus wide-eyed as he put his face in his hands and started crying in earnest. "What even the hell?"

"I think you should probably take him back home," Alma said. "Let him calm down and rest. And then talk, the two of you."

Terry turned to look at her. "Yes, you're right," she said, nodding weakly and rising to her feet. "How much—"

"We'll discuss payment at a later time," Alma cut her off. "Now is clearly not a good moment."

"But—"

"*Go*," Alma said firmly.

Gus was almost limp as Terry and Alma ushered him back down the corridor and through the front room, and he complied numbly when Terry put him in the car and told him to fasten his seat belt. In less than five minutes they were off, heading home.

Alma watched the car as it disappeared past a bend in the street. She walked all the way back to her inner sanctum and slowly, methodically, put everything back in its place, dragging the heavy chairs back around the table. Then she checked all parts of the theatrics — the fog machine, the small electrical motors on the curtains and the doors, and the carefully-aimed UV laser hidden in the rafters which had made the fluorescent crystal sphere light up — and did some light maintenance on them, to ensure they would be ready for the next client.

And then, when she'd exhausted the things which could distract her mind from what had just happened, she slumped down in a chair and sighed deeply. She'd said the words she was supposed to say, but Gus's reaction had been…unexpected. She hadn't thought he would take it quite that hard.

She shook her head.

She could only hope she hadn't screwed up a whole family's lives.

≡

As Terry was driving home, she kept sneaking glances at Gus, sitting beside her. He looked *terrible*. She'd never seen him like that. He almost looked as if his whole world had just come crashing down on him.

But why? Was Gus afraid Terry would leave him for a woman? Yes, that must've been it — that was the only thing that made sense. Nothing else Madame Alma had said had been out of the ordinary; there had been nothing in her words which could trigger such a reaction besides 'her mothers'.

But that was just absurd. Terry was bi, true — even though, in retrospect, she'd concluded that coming out to her (at the time future) husband and his parents had been a mistake, even if Gus, at least, had been accepting — but she wasn't *currently* in love with a woman; she was in love with *Gus*. And Gus knew that.

Didn't he?

Maybe he was unsure. After all, Madame Alma had proven that by channeling the spirits she could become privy to knowledge she shouldn't have been able to access otherwise; even Gus had clearly been convinced by what she'd told them about Dani. But that meant, however, that her words carried a heavy weight. What she'd said when she was doing the scrying...

Terry shook her head quickly to clear it. No. *No.* No way. Madame Alma must've been mistaken somehow. She'd interpreted the message the spirits had passed on to her in the wrong way.

Or maybe what she'd seen was just a *probable* future, and the *actual* future was yet to be written? Yes, that was the most likely explanation. After all, the spirits — an unseen, supernatural force — being able to gather information about the past or the present made sense: those events had already happened. But them being able to *predict the future?* The more Terry thought about it, the more she found the whole concept impossible. There were too many things which could change from one second to the next, too many variables.

So that must be it. The future isn't set in stone. In the end, it all comes down to what people choose.

Screw the occult. Screw the spirits. What did they even know, anyway? Terry would stand by her husband and help him with whatever it was he was going through and not run off with someone she didn't even love. Some *woman*.

She was going to talk with Gus, and tell him as much, as soon as they got home.

☰

Danielle looked up from her book when she heard the key turn in the lock and the door open. "Hey, welcome back!" She greeted her parents cheerfully before noticing the look in her mother's eyes and her father's slumped shoulders. He was looking at the floor and shuffling his feet, and he was barely moving by himself, letting Terry steer him around.

"What's wrong?" Dani asked, setting her book down and standing up from the couch. "Did something happen?"

Terry inclined her head. "Yes, you could say that. We..." She hesitated. "Your father and I need to have a talk. We'll be in our bedroom." She hesitated again. "You can fix dinner for yourself, right?"

"Yes, yes, I can," Dani nodded. "What happened?"

"I'll explain later."

Dani nodded again and watched as Terry gently pushed Gus into the bedroom and shut the door. She was about to get back to the couch, when the door opened again, and her mother stepped out and stood next to her.

"After we're done, I want to talk to you," Terry said in a hushed voice. Dani found herself answering in a whisper. "To me? About what?"

"Anything you may want to talk about. School, sports. Love troubles." Dani's eyebrows rose toward the ceiling while Terry continued, "If you don't want to say anything, it's okay. But I will listen if you do."

Terry put a hand on Dani's shoulder and squeezed it briefly. Then she walked back into the bedroom, pulling the door closed behind her.

≡

Terry leaned against the door and sighed. She looked down at Gus. She'd had him sit down on the bed while she left briefly to speak to Danielle, and he hadn't moved at all — he was still looking down at the floor, nearly in a daze. He'd stopped crying, at least.

She took a deep breath, crossed the small distance to the bed, and sat down next to him, passing an arm over his shoulders and pulling him close to her.

"Hey," she said. Gus didn't answer. After a moment, Terry squeezed his shoulder. "Do you wanna talk?" she asked. "If you don't want to, it's okay. You don't have to tell me anything. But I will listen if you do."

She felt Gus tense up, but then he relaxed again and whispered, "Taking Madame Alma's advice to heart, I see."

"Guilty as charged, I guess," Terry replied. "It is good advice, though."

"Yeah, it is," Gus said, nodding slightly.

After a moment of silence, Terry tried again. "So? Do you want to tell me anything?"

Gus sighed, exhaling all the air in his lungs, and as he did so he almost seemed to deflate. "What is there to say?" He asked. "I know you've got it all figured out."

It was Terry's turn to nod. "Yeah, I do. I know why you reacted the way you did."

"Alright. Then... Then I guess I'll take the couch for tonight."

Terry turned to him, frowning. "What?"

"I'll pack a few things and move out tomorrow," Gus continued, as if he hadn't heard Terry's question. "I'll come back for the rest eventually. Maybe."

Terry's frown deepened. "Gus. Gus, no," she said, shaking her head. "No, you don't have to move out."

"I don't?" Gus asked, looking at her in surprise.

"No, you don't. I don't want you to move out."

Gus kept looking at her for a moment, then shook his head. "I really should, though," he said. "I'll just get out of your hair. I won't even contest the divorce. This way, you'll be free to be with someone you truly love."

"No!" Terry shouted, standing up in a panic. "No, Gus! I don't want to be with someone else; I want to be with you!"

"Don't lie," Gus replied. "You can't love me. Not after... Not after what Madame Alma said."

"I'm not lying, Gus! I want to be with you!" She swallowed; her throat felt dry. "Even if Madame Alma said I would be happy with a woman, the future isn't set in stone. The future can change. So. Let's change it together. I want to be happy *with you*."

Gus kept looking down. He laughed bitterly. "You're right, the future isn't set in stone. That's why, no matter how much I wish for it, the future Madame Alma saw will never come true." He sighed. "I don't deserve you." He looked up at her, and there was an immense sadness in his eyes. "And you deserve to be with someone who hasn't been deceiving you all these years."

Terry blinked, taken aback. "Deceived? Gus, what are you saying?"

"You heard what that...that *witch* said, didn't you? 'Danielle and her mothers.' Don't even try to pretend you don't know what that means."

"I *do* know what that means! And I want to stay with you, despite Madame Alma's words!"

Gus shook his head again. "Please stop lying, Terry."

"I'm not lying!" Terry protested.

"You must be. After all..." He paused, his shoulders slumped, and he sighed. "Who would want to be with someone who has been pretending to be a man all this time?"

Terry felt her mouth fall open. She stared at Gus, speechless, trying to formulate words in her mind, to find an answer to what Gus had said. "What?" she finally managed, weak and barely audible. "You've been doing *what* all this time?"

"I thought about telling you so many times. *So* many times," Gus continued. "I mean, there shouldn't be secrets between spouses, right? Especially not secrets *this* big. I should've told you the moment you proposed to me. But in the end..." A deep sigh. "In the end, I just couldn't. Because...Well, I don't think you're transphobic, Terry. Not at all. But finding out your husband has been lying to you, ever since the day you met...I didn't think you would've been able to forgive *that*." Gus gulped. "I was selfish, I know. But I was afraid you'd leave me, so I just kept pushing the moment I would finally tell you back and back and back, and...and I ended up *not* telling you."

Terry could only stare as Gus stood up from the bed.

"But now that the secret is out..." Gus went on, walking to the door and opening it. "Well. Like I said, I guess I'll just get out of your hair."

Terry shook herself just as Gus was about to step out of the bedroom. No!

"No!" she shouted, surging forward and grabbing Gus's hand. "No. No, Gus. I don't want you to leave. I don't want to leave you, and I don't want you to leave me." She gulped. "Now sit back down."

Gus turned toward her in surprise. "But..."

"Sit *down*," Terry said firmly, tugging Gus back into the room and down onto the bed. Then she closed the door and took a deep breath.

And she started laughing.

"Oh my god!" she gasped. "This is...Oh my god! I was afraid you..."

She doubled over, laughing so hard she was unable to formulate any more words.

Gus frowned. "You were afraid I...What?"

Terry was still laughing. She held up a finger and then took a few seconds to compose herself.

"Okay!" She said, still giggling to herself. "Okay." She stepped forward and put her hands on Gus's shoulders. "My dear, from Madame Alma's words..." she began. "Well, I was afraid you would think I was going to leave you. After all... 'Danielle and her mothers.' The only way that could be true is if I were married to a woman. I was afraid you would think I was going to divorce you and marry someone else." She smiled. "But I *am* married to a woman, as it turns out. I'm married to you."

Gus stared at her, wide-eyed. "You're...You're not mad at me? You're not going to leave me?"

"Oh, I am *quite miffed* at you, my girl. Did you seriously think I'd be mad at you for being a woman? Honestly. Why did you hide yourself from me all this time? I have no idea. But no, I'm not going to leave you. Because I love you."

"You do?"

"I do," Terry answered. She leaned forward and gave Gus a peck on the lips which turned into a long, tender kiss — it was a minute or so before they came up for air.

"So!" She said brightly when she straightened up. "Have you given any thought about what you want to do regarding..." she waved in Gus's general direction, "This?"

Gus blinked. "Regarding what?"

"I mean, do you want to transition? Change your name? Or get on hormones? I mean, it's completely alright if you don't want to," Terry clarified, waving her hands in front of her. "It's a hundred percent your choice. I will support you either way. But I want to know. No more secrets."

"No more secrets," Gus replied nodding. "Okay. Well, there's...there's a name I like, actually. But I never thought I would ever get to use it."

Terry smiled warmly. "And that would be?"

Gus gulped. "Giselle."

"Well, nice to meet you again, Giselle! It's really a lovely name," Terry answered and wrapped her wife into a hug which lasted for several minutes.

"And also," Giselle continued, "I've thought about hormones before. I *wanted* hormones actually, but...there was just no way I could get on them. How could I ever hide them from you? Both the pills and the...effects."

"If you'd told me the truth in the first place, you wouldn't have to hide them," Terry chided her. "But yeah, hormones it is. And then clothes and a make-over...If you want that, of course. I'll follow your lead and help you along."

Giselle bit her lip, her face suddenly sad, and looked away.

"Giselle? Darling? What's wrong?" Terry asked.

"I..." Giselle said. "I want to do all that, but...What if I look ugly? I mean, I've been a man for nearly forty years."

Terry gently shook her head. "No, you've *looked like a man* for nearly forty years. It's only a matter of bringing out the inside and shaping the outside to match. And let me just say..."

She leaned forward, smiled warmly, and whispered conspiratorially, "I can already see it. You're going to be *so pretty*."

And despite everything that had happened, Giselle couldn't help but smile back.

≡

The phone barely rang once.

"Danielle," said the voice on the other end.

"Hi, Alma."

"How did it go?"

"Very well, actually! Everything is fine."

Alma sighed deeply. "Good. That's...great, actually. Sorry. I was afraid I'd screwed everything up."

"Don't worry, you didn't," Danielle replied. "My dad...Well, I guess she's not my dad, is she? My mom came out to me at dinner with my other mom's support." She smiled. "I pretended to be surprised."

"Do you think you're ever going to tell them?" Alma asked.

Unseen by her friend, Dani shrugged. "Eventually? Maybe? Probably after I move out for college. I mean, think about it. 'Hey Mom, hey Other Mom, listen to this: I figured out Other Mom was actually a closeted trans woman — *way* too knowledgeable about queer issues to be just a really good ally, and I saw her dressed up once when I came home unexpectedly — and then I snuck into her bedroom and read her private diary to make sure, and *then* when you two told me you wanted to talk to a medium I made an appointment with a queer friend of mine. Oh, and I told her exactly what to say to push my mom out of the closet'? That would get me grounded for *centuries*."

Alma laughed. "It would, yes. Best not to tell them for a while yet. Exactly how much of what you told me to say was true?"

"About half. I *am* being bullied, and I *am* having love troubles, and I *am* concerned about my fitness. But I can handle all that by myself. The bad grades, though, those were on purpose, to make my moms concerned enough to seek help for me." Dani paused. "And I sabotaged every other meeting they'd had until they came to you. I'm really grateful for your help, by the way. Couldn't have done it without you."

"I'm sure you'd have thought of something," Alma answered. "But if you need me again in the future, you just need to ask. I'll gladly do some theatrics if that's what's needed to crack a few eggs."

"Thank you, girl. You're the best."

"Hey, that's what friends are for, aren't they? And if that's not enough, we'll ask the spirits for help."

The Princess and Her Hunter

THE FIRST TIME their eyes meet, they're sitting across from each other in a wide circle of trans and non-binary people. They each study the other for a moment then smile in recognition of their kinship.

"Good evening, everyone, and welcome to our bi-weekly trans support group meeting," James says, clapping his hands. "Today we have two new people who've moved into town recently, so I think we can start with them. Want to introduce yourself? Name, pronouns, age, and an interesting fact about yourself, just to start us off."

"I'm—" Faye begins.

"My name—" Maddie starts at the same time.

The two girls stop speaking. They glance at each other then they burst out laughing.

"Enthusiastic, aren't we?" James says, joining in the laugh. "Alright. Maddie, you go first."

Maddie nods. "I'm Madeline. Maddie. Nice to meet y'all. I'm twenty-four, my pronouns are she and her, and…Let's see…I get sunburned very easily?"

"That's to be expected," Faye says with a grin. "You are a shade of white between milk and snow."

"Got something against pale girls?" Maddie asks with a mild smile.

Faye shakes her head. "No, not at all, just making an observation. And you look super good." Maddie rewards her with a bright smile which makes Faye's heart skip a beat and her cheeks turn pink. It takes her a moment to realize James is looking at her expectantly. "Right, okay. Hi everyone, I'm Faye. I'm also twenty-four and my pronouns are also she and her, and I like sports. Both watching and playing."

"I could tell," Maddie says. "Even with those loose clothes you're wearing, I can see you're in good shape."

"It's difficult to stay in shape once you've reached it, though," Faye says. "You should know; you're very fit, too."

Maddie shakes her head. "It's just my natural body shape, I hardly ever exercise."

"Huh. Damn, girl, what's your secret? I'd give an arm to look half as good as you do," Faye replies, and this time it's Maddie who blushes and looks away.

James coughs discreetly. "Alright, if you two are quite done…?" When Maddie and Faye both nod, he continues. "Okay then. Now it's everyone else's turn to introduce themselves, and then we can get the discussion started. Phil?"

≡

"Alright, and that's all the time we have for today," James says, clapping his hands again. "As usual, we're going to the bar just down the street for a drink. Anyone is welcome to join. For everyone else, the next meeting is in two weeks, same weekday, same bat-time, same bat-channel."

Everybody gets up from their chairs and stretches a bit, driving the kinks of a few hours spent sitting out of their limbs. Maddie exchanges a few words with the girl and enby who were sitting right next to her then she crosses the circle and approaches Faye. "Faye, right?" she says, holding out her hand.

"Yes. And you're Madeline," Faye replies, shaking it.

"Maddie."

They keep looking at each other for a long moment, still holding each other's hand, and then finally let go. "So," Maddie asks, "are you coming to the bar?"

"I'm not sure," Faye says, shaking her head. "I'm not much of a drinker, really. I find that alcohol dulls my reflexes a bit too much."

"I don't think that would be a problem," Maddie says. "They're bound to have something fruity you can drink instead. Right?" she adds, turning toward James, who looks briefly away from his own conversation to nod and give them a thumbs-up. She turns back toward Faye. "See?

And even if you don't find anything that suits your tastes, you can just have water and enjoy the company."

Faye raises an eyebrow. "*Your* company?"

"If you want," Maddie says, shrugging.

≡

"Are you sure you don't want to taste this?" Maddie asks, motioning with her glass. "It's good."

Faye takes the drink from her, gives it a sniff, and makes a face. "Ugh. No, thank you, I'm good."

"Suit yourself." Maddie accepts the glass back, takes a long sip, and sets the beer down on the counter. They're sitting away from the rest of the group. The bar didn't have a large enough table for them all, so they decided to sacrifice themselves.

"I don't know how you do it," Faye says. "I mean, there's *some* booze I like, but beer? Especially IPAs? Dear God, no. Too hoppy for my tastes."

"So, what do you drink?" Maddie asks.

"Mixed drinks, mostly," Faye replies. "Radlers, sometimes."

"What's a radler?"

"Beer mixed with citrus juice. And above all, I don't like tannins, so I definitely don't drink…wine."

Maddie blinks. The way Faye paused before the final word…

"Not even under torture? I mean, if someone pointed a stake at you," Maddie says and watches as Faye's eyebrows lift slightly toward the ceiling, "and forced you to pick between a Merlot or a Cabernet or a Pinot Noir, which would you choose?"

Faye looks at Maddie warily. Then, carefully, she replies, "I'd let them drive that stake right through my heart."

There's a moment of silence as they look at each other. They both smile.

"How long have you known?" Faye asks.

"Since the beginning, I think?" Maddie says. "I kinda got *that feeling* from you when I first saw you at the group. You?"

"Same. I don't think anyone else noticed, but for people like us, we can just tell, right?"

"Right. But you still took a big risk by making a fang joke to confirm it. We're not all super friendly. Lots of rivalries going around." Maddie scoffs. "My dad absolutely doesn't want me to socialize, but that's *dumb*. We're a community, aren't we? We're all in the same boat."

"Yeah. Strength in numbers. Especially since we have to face what's out there hunting us." Faye takes a deep gulp of her fruity drink and then continues, "But it doesn't matter to me. I left that life behind when I ran away from home."

Maddie bumps her shoulder against Faye's. "Wanna tell me about it?"

"No," Faye replies. "Not right now. It's a nice moment, let's not dwell on the past."

"Alright."

"But I'm going to say one thing."

Maddie turns to face Faye, a questioning look in her eyes.

"I'm happy to have met someone who's like me in more ways than one," Faye says, smiling at Maddie.

Maddie smiles back. "You got that right, sister."

They lean into each other and clink their glasses together.

※

"Are you sure you're alright?" Faye asks, handing Maddie a bottle of ice-cold water.

"Yeah, I'm fine," Maddie says, taking the drink and pressing it against her forehead. She's sitting in the shade of a gazebo, away from the scorching light of the August sun. "Thanks. I'll just sit here for a while until I cool down a bit, and then we can move on."

"You could've told me you're bad with the heat," Faye says. "We could've gone somewhere else."

Maddie looks up at her and smiles a tired smile. "Yeah, but…you know. You were so enthusiastic about the theme park, I wanted to see what makes this place so special to you."

Faye blushes a bit and smiles back. "Thanks," she says, and sits down on the bench next to Maddie.

They're quiet for a long time, just enjoying each other's company, while Maddie sips on the water. "Okay, I'm good," she finally says. "So, what do you want to do now?"

"There's a part that's entirely in the shade," Faye says. "They set up a big circus tent, like a big top, and they have stuff in there that you would find in county fairs. You know, ring tossing, shooting galleries, that kind of thing."

"Sounds fun," Maddie says, rising to her feet. "Let's go."

Faye stands up too, takes Maddie by the hand, and leads her partway across the park to a large tent. As they make their way inside, Maddie marvels at the various stands — it's really fascinating, everything is in kind of a retro style, almost a throwback to the 1950s.

"Well, hello, ladies," a man's voice says. "What are two beautiful girls like you doing all on your own?"

Maddie and Faye both frown at the guy approaching them. From the way he swaggers, he looks like he thinks he owns the place. "Hi," Faye says evenly. "Can we help you?"

"Well, maybe I can help *you*," he says. "I'd like to offer you two a drink, what do you say?"

Maddie shakes her head. "I'm going to stop you right there and avoid disappointing you," she says. "You should probably know that the two of us are currently on a date."

The guy's smile doesn't falter. "Well then, are you sure you wouldn't like to go on a date with *me* rather than with each other?"

"Not interested," Maddie replies while Faye shakes her head.

"Oh, come on, sweethearts," he insists, "are you *sure*?"

Faye's eyes narrow. She looks away from the guy for a moment, gazing around the space inside the tent, and then looks back at him. "Tell you what, I'm going to make you a bet. You see the high ringer over there?"

She points, and the man turns to look. "Yeah, what about it?" he asks.

"If I beat you at that, you'll leave us alone. Deal?"

He grins. "Deal."

They make their way over to the attraction, where the barker is waving his cane around — Maddie has to giggle: it really *is* a throwback

— and shouting, "Come one, come all! Let's see who is a boy and who's a man! Step right up! You win a stuffed animal if you can ring the bell!"

The guy swaggers up to the barker, pays him the required five dollars, and grabs the heaviest mallet, the one which weighs twenty pounds. He feels the weight a bit then, with a fluid movement, he raises it high and brings it down on the lever.

"Ooh, about two thirds of the way to the top!" the barker says. "Not bad! So, who's up next?"

"Go ahead," the guy says, motioning for Faye to have her turn.

Her face neutral, Faye steps up, hands the barker a fiver, and lifts the mallet with one hand, seemingly without effort. She looks at it for a moment, turning it back and forth. "Huh. Heavier than I thought," she says.

Maddie giggles as everyone else's eyes go wide.

Faye smirks and slams the mallet down.

The bell goes *ding*.

"Oh, Faye, you're *so strong!*" Maddie squeals and gives Faye a hug. Faye smiles at her, takes the plushie from the astonished barker, and offers it to Maddie with a bow.

"For you, my princess," she says.

"Why, thank you."

"Wh— How? You cheated!" the guy says, recovering from his shock. "There's no way you could...You *cheated!*"

"I did not. And even if I did, a bet's a bet, right?" Faye says.

"You didn't win, you—" he begins.

"Want to make another bet?" Maddie says and steps up to a nearby booth. "How about knife throwing?"

She hands a fiver to the attendant, grabs the five knives he hands her, and throws four of them in quick succession at the target, ten feet away: four bullseyes.

She turns around and looks at the guy, raising the last knife and smiling sweetly. "Want to see what else I can do with a knife?" she asks.

He blinks at her. Then, after a moment, he turns around and runs away.

Faye and Maddie exchange a glance and then break out into a giggling fit.

"So, what's so special about this place?" Faye asks as Maddie pulls her into the diner, the bell above the door dinging to announce their entrance. "Looks like a normal diner."

"It is a normal diner, but I come here when I want to relax," Maddie says. "The owner's very friendly, and he took a liking to me right away. Oh, and the scrambled eggs are good." She turns around and calls out, "Hey! Boss!"

A man peeks his head out of a door, smiling when he sees them. "Oh, hi Maddie!" he says. "Give me a sec, I'll finish cutting these peppers, and I'll be right there."

It takes less than a minute for him to fully emerge from the door, and when he does Faye is seriously impressed. He's as tall and wide as a wardrobe and looks like he could bench-press a car. He smiles kindly down at her as he holds out his hand. "Hi, I'm Dave, but you can call me Boss," he says.

"Faye," Faye says, shaking his hand. "I'm Maddie's friend."

Boss inclines his head to the side and gives her a skeptical look. "Friend?"

"Friend." Faye nods.

"Alright, if you say so," he says, shrugging. "Now what can I do for ya?"

"Dinner would be nice," Maddie says.

"Take a seat wherever you like," Boss says, waving his hand to encompass the inside of the diner. It's a bit late in the evening — Maddie and Faye had been to the movies — so there are just a few people there. "I'll tell Anya to bring you a menu."

Maddie nods and leads Faye to a table off to the side, next to the window. "This is my favorite spot. You can see the cars go by," she says. "And when it rains, the water beads up on the glass, scattering the light."

"It's a nice place," Faye says.

"Isn't it? I found it by chance when I first came to town. I had no place to go, and Boss was kind enough to let me sleep on one of the lounge chairs for the night. Then, the next day, he called up a friend and got me a place to stay."

"Huh. I'll have to thank him," Faye says.

"What for?"

"Because if you didn't have a place to stay, you probably would've moved on to another city, and then we wouldn't have met," Faye says, smiling warmly at Maddie.

Maddie smiles back and squeezes Faye's hand.

"Here you are, ladies," the waitress says, setting the menus down on the table. "Oh, hi Maddie!"

"Hi, Anya," Maddie greets her. "How's life?"

"Good, good. Me and my partners are thinking about moving in together, so."

"Oh, that's great!"

Anya nods. "It is. How about you? Anyone new in your life?"

Her eyes wander to Faye, and Maddie giggles. "Probably, yeah," she says.

"Good for you two. I'll leave you to decide," Anya says, starting to walk away.

"Oh, can you bring us some garlic bread to start us off?" Maddie calls after her.

"You got it!" Anya calls back, half-turning toward them. As she does so, she inadvertently bumps a man who's standing next to the diner's counter, making him drop his glass. It crashes to the ground and shatters loudly.

"What the fuck! Watch where the hell you're going!" The man shouts.

"Oh, Lord, I'm sorry," Anya says, taking a step back.

"Sorry doesn't cut it!" The man rebuts loudly. "You made me spill my drink! What are you going to do about that?"

Maddie and Faye both frown. Maddie stands up.

"I'll bring you another one," Anya says.

"One isn't enough! I need at least two!" He takes a step toward her, and she steps back again. "Or three more! You hear that, you bitch?"

"Yes, I hear that," Anya mumbles, taking another step back. "I…I'll go and get a broom and clean this up." She turns around, hurriedly walking toward the double doors to the kitchen.

"Wait, where the hell do you think you're—" the man says and is about to start after her, but he's interrupted when a hand lands on his shoulder, and he whirls around to face Maddie.

"Dude, what the hell are you doing?" Maddie asks. "Can't you see you're scaring her?"

"Damn right I'm scaring her!" The man exclaims. "That bitch made me spill my drink! She ought to be scared!"

Faye steps up next to Maddie. "Listen, buddy, you don't want to be doing this."

"I don't want to be doing *what?*" The man shouts, and by now, everyone in the diner is looking at the unfolding scene. "I don't want to be putting you bitches in your place?"

"No. Seriously, you're making a scene," Faye says, and she steps back and raises her hands.

Maddie nods and imitates her. "Let's just all take a deep breath and don't do anything we might regret."

The man, however, is either too drunk or too stupid — or maybe both — to be reasonable. His face red, he shouts, "I'm not regretting, you're gonna be regretting!" And he squares up. "Come at me, bitches!"

"I've got a different idea," a deep voice says, and Boss steps out of the kitchen and up to the group. "Why don't you leave the ladies alone and fuck off out of my restaurant?"

The man glances at him, pales, and gulps. "I…I'm sorry," he stammers, staring up at Boss. "I was just…"

"Nope, don't wanna hear it," Boss says. "But I'll be generous and not make you pay for what you've drunk and eaten as long as you fuck off right this moment. Deal?"

The drunkard hurriedly leaves without as much as a look behind. Boss exhales, and suddenly he's standing differently. He's far less menacing than he was just a moment before. "You gals alright?" He asks.

"Yeah, we are," Faye says, and Maddie dips her chin in agreement.

"Want anything to drink? On the house." The two girls both shake their heads, and Boss nods in return. "I'll bring a broom and clean the mess up." He turns around and walks away.

Faye crouches down to the floor and starts picking up the largest pieces of the shattered glass.

"You alright?" Maddie asks, crouching down next to her.

"Yeah," Faye exhales slowly. "Yeah, I'm alright. I was a bit nervous, but between the two of us, we could have more than taken him had it come to that."

Maddie nods. "Right. We're not normal people, after all."

"Yeah, and— *Fuck*," Faye swears, and her hand snaps back.

"What is it?"

"Cut myself," Faye says, pointing to her fingertip, where a bead of deep red blood is forming. "Guess I was too focused on your eyes."

Maddie groans and rolls the eyes in question. "Oh, you. Give that here."

Before Faye has time to protest, Maddie's grabbed her hand and put Faye's finger in her mouth. Faye's eyes go wide. "Maddie…"

"Shush," Maddie mumbles, sucking softly. Then she smiles. "You taste good."

Faye blushes deeply, so deep it's clearly visible even on her dark skin. "I…" she begins.

"Should you really be doing this right here, right now?" Boss's voice says, and when the two girls look up, he's looking down at them, a broom and dustpan in his hands and an eyebrow raised.

Maddie and Faye look at him then at each other then back up at him. "Probably not?" Faye says, and she reluctantly pulls back her hand. Maddie shrugs and smiles sheepishly.

Boss chuckles. "Go back to your table, ladies, and let me work."

≡

"Hi, Maddie," Faye says, waving as she sees Maddie round the corner.

"Hi," Maddie replies, and she leans forward to hug Faye. "Are you all set?"

"Of course. I've got movie tickets, and I've made dinner reservations."

"Oh? Where?"

"Where else?" Faye grins. "At Boss's diner."

Maddie smiles back. "Alright, let's go."

Chatting, they start making their way from the bus station to the movie theater. As they do so, they cut through the back of a construction site. Before they reach the street a man steps out of the shadows to bar their way.

They stop walking and frown at him. "What do you want?" Faye asks.

"You," the man replies, pointing at her. "You're coming with me, boy. As for you, girl," he adds, pointing at Maddie, "fuck off, and I won't hurt you."

Faye frowns. It's been a while since she's last been misgendered, and this man acts as if he knows her. "No fucking way. I'm not coming with you," she says.

"And I'm not leaving," Maddie adds.

"Have it your way," the man says, and he springs forward, toward Maddie.

Startled, Maddie steps back, quickly falling into a defensive position, while Faye steps forward and lashes out with her fist, carefully controlling her strength: she doesn't want to kill this guy if she can help it.

The punch connects with the man's arm as he shields himself from Faye's blow. He barely flinches, and Faye frowns — he's sturdier than she thought. She steps forward, following him, and brings her leg around at head height. The man parries the blow once again, but Faye's put more power into it, and there's a crunching sound as his arm snaps. Faye's foot connects with his temple, and he falls to the ground, apparently out cold.

Faye breathes out as she steadies herself and gulps a couple times. It's been a while since she's had to properly fight. She turns back toward Maddie.

"Are you okay?" Maddie asks.

"Yeah, I'm alright," Faye replies with a nod. "That was weird. It was almost as if—"

"Faye, look out!" Maddie shouts as the man gets to his feet with surprising speed, right behind Faye. Faye whirls around to face him, bringing her hands up to parry his blow. But he's not going for a punch: he's grasped her and pulled her close.

"Why, you..." Faye grits out as she grapples with him. He's *really* strong, much stronger than a normal human. Trying to get herself in a position where she can pull him to the ground, she shifts her footing and moves slightly to the side.

And that gives Maddie a clear shot.

The sharpened stake sinks deep into the man's chest, a fraction of an inch from his heart. He gasps for breath, but it's only a moment before Faye instinctively takes advantage of the opening and sinks her fangs into his neck, and a couple seconds more before she's fully drained him. He crumples to the ground in a desiccated heap, but neither girl is paying attention to him any longer.

They're both standing incredibly still, and it takes them a few moments before they fully realize what's happened and piece the sequence of events together.

Maddie looks at the twin holes on the man's neck. Faye looks at the stake piercing the man's heart.

Maddie, wide-eyed, stares at Faye. Faye, wide-eyed, stares at Maddie.

"You're a *vampire?!*" Maddie exclaims.

"You're a *hunter?!*" Faye shouts at the same time.

They both blink in surprise.

"Of *course* I'm a hunter," Maddie says. "I thought you were a hunter, too!"

"And *I* thought *you* were a vampire!" Faye rebuts. "When were you going to tell me you're not?"

"Uh, *never*? Because I thought we'd understood each other when we first met? You know, that thing you told me? 'I'm happy to meet someone who's like me in more ways than one?' I thought you meant you were glad to meet another hunter!"

"No, I meant I was glad to meet another vampire!" Faye pauses. "Wait, if you're not a vampire, what the fuck was that back at the diner? You sucking the blood off my finger?"

"It's called *flirting*, you dumb walnut!"

"I know what flirting is, I thought it was something more! Just FYI, sharing blood is a *very* intimate thing among vampires!"

Maddie blinks, taken aback. "Is it?"

"It is! It's basically the equivalent of a proposal!"

"Why didn't you tell me?!"

"I thought you *knew!*"

Maddie stares at Faye for a moment then lets out an exasperated sigh and shakes her head. "God, I can't fucking believe this. My girlfriend's a vampire."

Faye blinks. "Wait, I'm still your girlfriend?!"

"Not the point! I mean..." Maddie pauses, shakes her head again, then continues, "Well, it kinda *is* the point, isn't it? I've been trained to hunt vampires all my life. I've been trained to *hate* vampires all my life. And now..."

"Okay, two can play at this game. *I've* been trained to hate *hunters* all my life. And besides, why do you hunt us anyway?"

"Because you're vampires? You kill people."

Faye hesitates for a moment and bites her lip. "Okay, point taken, my relatives *do* kill people. But I don't."

Maddie glances at the dried-out corpse lying on the ground next to Faye's feet. "Um," she says.

"Except in self-defense," Faye adds. "And besides, he wasn't a person any longer; he was a thrall. It means—"

"A human who willingly serves a vampire in exchange for being allowed to drink vampire blood, which stops them from aging and grants them great strength and perfect health." Maddie nods. "I know. Hunter, remember?" She pauses for a moment, and then, surprisingly, she giggles. "Wait, I never put it together, but does this mean that you steal men's souls and make them your slaves?"

"Har har har, laugh it up," Faye replies, but she's smiling. "This guy was probably one of my dad's, I recognize the stench."

"Your dad? You mean your sire?"

"No, I mean my dad. I was born a vampire, not made one."

Maddie gasps in surprise. "Wait, you're a Daylight Walker? A fucking *Great Ancient?*"

"I'm a Daylight Walker, yes, and that explains how I can walk around during the day, doesn't it?" Faye says with a grin, and Maddie realizes it's true — she's been so caught up in the moment she hadn't remembered that she has had many a date with Faye in full sunlight. "But don't call me ancient. My dad's ancient. I'm twenty-four."

"Are you really?" Maddie asks, looking at her skeptically.

"I'm not lying, I really am twenty-four. In the grand scheme of things I'm a wee little baby, even though my dad's one of the oldest vampires around."

"So, you're the *daughter* of a Great Ancient. Whoa," Maddie breathes out. "My girlfriend's a bloody vampire princess."

Faye doesn't mention that Maddie has used the g-word again; she just chuckles. "That I am. But wait," she adds with a frown, "how do you know about Daylight Walkers? We're supposed to be a secret. Very hush hush, no one knows about us, not even hunters, usually."

"That's because..." Maddie says. Then, after a pause, she sighs. "You see, when I say I'm a hunter, I mean that with a capital H. It's even my surname, Hunter. Our family is one of the oldest still around. My ancestors have been hunting vampires for millennia, quite literally. We're very respected in the...the *community*, and we know some things other hunters don't." She pauses again. "It's a lot of pressure, you know?"

"Yes, I can see how that would be," Faye says. "You're supposed to carry on the family business, right?"

"Right. But...only boys can inherit. It's *tradition*, you see," Maddie says, quirking her mouth in distaste. "And my dad...Well, he's old and *stubborn*, and he doesn't like that I'm a girl. So, I ran away."

"Oh. Like I did," Faye says.

"Right, I remember you telling me about that."

Faye nods. "I was literally conceived because my dad wanted an heir. And, well, because of *tradition*, that heir has to be a man, and my dad, like yours, doesn't accept that I'm a girl."

"Oh," Maddie says, blinking in realization. "That's why he sent his thrall after you."

"Yeah, probably." Faye sighs. "I'll have to move, since my dad clearly knows where I am."

She looks at Maddie. Maddie looks back at her.

"So. What do *we* do now?" Faye asks.

Maddie bites her lip pensively. "Well, you're a vampire. A Daylight Walker, even. And I'm a capital-H Hunter. By all rights, we should fight each other."

"But you don't want to."

"You're right, I don't."

"Well, I don't, either. So, I think I'll just leave."

Faye makes to turn around but stops when Maddie calls out for her to wait. They look at each other for a moment then Maddie takes a deep breath and lets it out. "If you're leaving, I'm coming with you. Wherever you want to go."

"Are you sure?"

"I am. I've never been more sure in my entire life."

Faye looks at Maddie for a few seconds then nods. She steps over the thrall's body, quickly covering the short distance that separates her from Maddie. Maddie knows she should feel afraid — there's a Daylight Walker! Right there! Moving purposefully toward her! — but somehow, she doesn't, and she stands rooted in place as Faye stops right in front of her, their faces inches apart.

They stare into each other's eyes for a long moment.

"Stakes can't kill me. Just by the way," Faye says.

Maddie's eyebrows rise toward the sky. "They can't?"

"Nope," Faye says, putting her hands on Maddie's waist and drawing her even closer. "Wood stakes work fine against normal vampires, and they do sting a bit, but you need silver or fire, or both, if you want to put a Daylight Walker down for the count."

"Why are you telling me this?" Maddie asks, though she feels as if she already knows the answer.

Faye smiles. "Because I want my girlfriend to trust me. And because I trust my girlfriend enough to know that she won't shank me while I'm sleeping."

"I promise I won't," Maddie says, reciprocating the smile. "As long as you promise not to bite me without permission."

"I promise I won't."

They lean in, and they kiss.

The bell above the door dings as Faye and Maddie enter the diner, shaking the rain off themselves. "Oh, hel...lo?" Boss says, frowning at them. "What's wrong? You don't look so good."

"Boss, we...we came to say goodbye," Maddie says.

His frown deepens. "Goodbye?"

Maddie swallows hard. "We're leaving. This is the last time we'll see you."

"Oh. Where are you going?"

"Away. We don't know where yet."

Boss looks at them for a moment then nods. "Alright, girls, take a seat. You gotta eat before leaving, right?"

Faye hesitates. "But..."

"*Sit*," Boss repeats. Then, more softly, he adds, "Please?"

"Alright," Maddie says, and Faye nods. They take a seat at their favorite table and talk in hushed tones, glancing outside through the window beaded with rain. The storm rages on outside as Boss walks off to the kitchen. He's back in short order with two bowls of chili con carne.

"On the house," he says, sitting down at the table with them. "Eat up."

The girls dig in, attacking the chili with spoons and gusto, and Boss looks at them for a moment. Then he reaches out and places a circular silver token, about an inch across, down on the table. The visible face is decorated with an elaborate emblem.

Maddie blinks at the item then looks up at Boss with wide eyes. "Boss...?" she whispers.

"Do you want to go somewhere else?" Boss asks quietly.

Maddie holds his gaze for a moment then shakes her head. "No, right here is okay," she says.

"Maddie, what's this about?" Faye asks.

"That token is our badge," Maddie explains, looking at Faye. "It's a way to recognize each other without any need for words." She looks at Boss again. "So. You're a hunter."

"I am," Boss replies. "With a capital H, too. You and I are third cousins once removed. I've been trained, but I'm not really in the business, I just offer logistical support. When you ran away from home your dad had you followed and, when it became clear you'd settled here, he called and asked me to keep an eye on you."

"Why would he do that?" Maddie asks.

"Because he thought...How did he put it? He said that you would come to your senses soon enough, put this whole 'being a girl' nonsense behind you, and come back home." He pauses and then, carefully, he adds, "Apparently, he's changed his mind, because a few hours ago I got a phone call from him. He told me to *bring* you back home. By any means necessary."

Maddie and Faye both tense up. Faye's lips start to draw back to expose her teeth, while Maddie tightens her grip on the spoon. It's not much of a weapon, but it's still solid metal, and—

"Relax," Boss says, raising a hand. "I ain't doing that."

Faye narrows her eyes at him. "Again: why?"

"Because I'm not an ass-backwards bigoted fuck like he is. You deserve to live your life how you wish, *as who* you wish, without anyone telling you otherwise."

"Thank you," Maddie says with a smile.

Boss nods. "Unfortunately, your dad will stop at nothing to bring you back. And believe me, he's very well connected. There's nowhere you can go he'll be unable to find you."

Maddie slumps in her seat. "Oh. So, what do I do? What do *we* do?" she asks, exchanging a glance with Faye.

"Okay, first of all," Boss says, "we've been having this discussion in front of Faye here and I can't help but notice she's been entirely unsurprised by the whole thing, so she obviously knows about you. But do *you* know about *her*?"

"She knows," Faye says. "I've told her who I am." Maddie nods.

"Okay. Then I won't need this." Boss reaches down and, with a sharp movement, unhooks something from his belt and sets it squarely down on the table. It's a silver knife, a menacing stiletto, the blade six inches long. Faye looks at it and hisses. "Yeah, sorry for bringing a Hunter blade to the table," Boss adds, "but I wanted to be prepared in case things got ugly. Believe me, I'm *really* glad I don't have to use this. I like you, Faye."

"Hold on," Faye says. "I've just put the dots together just now. How did you know about me, exactly?"

"Maddie's dad told me."

"Okay. And how did *he* know about me?"

"He knows about you because he's working with your dad."

Faye and Maddie both blink. "Wait, *what?*" Maddie exclaims. "Our dads are working together?!"

"They are," Boss says. "Daylight Walkers and capital-H Hunters have been working together for nearly a millennium. We have an agreement of sorts: Hunters tolerate a certain amount of dead humans and refrain from attacking Daylight Walkers directly. Daylight Walkers, on the other hand, don't go around siring too many vampires and likewise don't attack us Hunters directly." He pauses. "And they also agree on other things."

"Such as?" Maddie asks.

"How old is your dad, Maddie?"

Maddie inclines her head and gives him a curious look. "I don't know? I've never thought about it. He looks like he's in his mid-forties, probably."

"And how long has he looked like he's in his mid-forties?"

"...Ever since I was old enough to remember, actually," Maddie answers, eyes narrowing. "You mean...?"

"Oh yeah. Faye's dad has been providing your dad with vampire blood for centuries now. My guess is that they don't want to risk another Hunter taking over, which would upset the balance. And, speaking of which, it's no coincidence your dads both decided to father heirs twenty-four years ago. It was so you would both succeed them at the same time and keep the agreement going."

"Huh," Faye says. Then she bursts into giggles.

"What's up?" Maddie says.

Faye shakes her head. "Nothing, it's just...I think it's a bit ironic. The two of us were literally meant to be together, right from the start."

"Well, not *together* together," Boss says, "but more or less, yeah."

"So, it's destiny. We were destined to meet each other," Maddie says, looking at Faye and smiling. Faye beams back.

They gaze into each other's eyes for a few long moments before Boss coughs discreetly. "Let's not get sidetracked here, girls."

"Sorry." Maddie blushes. Faye shrugs sheepishly.

"So, now that we're all on the same page, here comes the million-dollar question: what do we do?" Boss asks.

Maddie inclines her head to the side and hums pensively. "I think I know what to do, actually. I think I have a plan."

"You do?"

"Yeah," Maddie nods, and she reaches out and grabs Faye's hand, giving it a squeeze. "I think it's time for you to go home."

≡

After taking a deep breath, Faye pushes open the doors to the mansion and walks in. "Father," she announces loudly. "I have returned."

It takes a few moments for the echoes of her voice to die down and about a minute before her dad appears at the top of the staircase.

"Son," he says evenly, looking down at her. "I have to admit, I did not expect you to come back of your own volition. Especially not after what you did to poor Baldwin."

"Was that the name of the thrall you sent after me?" Faye says. "If so, my apologies for draining him. But he could've explained his intent better."

"He had, admittedly, a tendency to rush into things," the Great Ancient says dryly. Then, after a pause, he continues, "Have you finally come to your senses?"

Faye bobs her head up and down. "I have. I'm ready to take my place by your side as your heir. And to prove it, I have brought you a gift."

She steps briefly back outside, and roughly pulls Maddie, who's tied up and gagged, into view before pushing her inside, making her fall to the floor in a kneeling position.

"Behold," Faye says. "The child of your enemy."

Faye's father regards them for a moment and then nods. "Very well. Kill him."

Without hesitating for even a moment, Faye plunges her fangs into Maddie's neck. After a couple seconds, Maddie crumples to the ground.

Faye wipes away a rivulet of blood from the corner of her mouth and spreads her arms, looking up expectantly at her father.

"You have done well, my son," he says. "Clearly—"

"What is the *meaning of this!*" A voice says, and a middle-aged man storms into the mansion, followed closely by Boss. "You! Beast!" the man shouts, pointing at the Great Ancient. "What have you done to my son? I thought we had an agreement!"

"Hunter," the vampire says. "What are you doing here?"

"My cousin told me what was happening, and I rushed over. I thought we had an agreement!"

The Great Elder hesitates for a moment then shakes his head. "It was not I who did this. My son did it without my permission."

Faye blinks and looks at him. "Father?!" she exclaims.

"I hope this...*unfortunate* misunderstanding does not alter the terms of our agreement," Faye's father continues, ignoring his daughter.

The Hunter chews on the inside of his cheek for a moment. "No," he carefully decides. "No, I think not. I have lost a son, true, but I can father another one. A better one. One who's not a sissy like he was." He pauses. "But I demand satisfaction. I demand your son's life in return."

"Take it," the Great Ancient says without a moment's hesitation.

"Father!" Faye shouts. "Don't do this! I am your son!"

"I can father another one," the vampire says. "A better one."

The Hunter nods in approval and steps toward Faye.

"Alright, I think that's enough," Faye says. "It's clear you're a pair of irredeemable jerks. What do you think, Maddie?"

In one fluid movement Maddie rolls over and stands, the ropes coming untied with a tug and falling to the ground around her feet. "I think you're right, Faye," she says after removing her gag.

Their fathers' eyes go wide. "It was a ruse?" the vampire asks.

"Yup, sure was," Faye says. "We already knew how you two felt about us, but we wanted to see what your reaction would be to us being placed in mortal danger."

"Just for the record, that reaction was *not good*," Maddie says.

Faye nods. "You both get an F."

There's a moment of silence then the Hunter says, "So now you know. What are you going to do about it?"

"What do you think?" Maddie says. "Hey, Drac, think fast."

Her arm moves in a flash, and six inches of silver sail through the air and embed themselves into the Great Ancient's heart. He only has time to gasp before he explodes into dust.

The Hunter blinks and then he smiles. "My son! Well done! I'm—"

"Nope," Faye says. "Absolutely not. Sorry, but you're not getting off the hook that easily."

"What do you mean?"

"I mean that Maddie has taken care of my idiot father for me. And now I get to take care of *her* idiot father for her."

Faye steps toward the Hunter. He blinks in surprise and tries to take a step back, but Boss is standing right behind him, and he grabs his arms, pinning him in a hold.

"David!" the Hunter demands, struggling uselessly against him. "What in the hell are you *doing?*"

"Helping out my friends," Boss says. "Go ahead, Faye."

Faye is next to them in the blink of an eye. The Hunter's scream is cut short, and, when Boss lets him go, he falls to the ground, drained of blood.

"Phew," Faye says, wiping her lips. Then she turns toward Maddie. "Are you alright?" she asks. "I didn't drink too much, did I? I'm so sorry about biting you, I had to do it to sell the whole thing."

"Don't worry," Maddie says, walking up to her and putting her hands on Faye's hips. "I'm perfectly okay." She pauses. "Do I taste good?"

Faye giggles. "You taste *delicious*."

They lean in, and kiss deeply. Eventually, Boss loudly clears his throat.

"Oh, shush," Maddie says, and Faye sticks her tongue out at him.

"So, regarding the next part of our plan," Boss says. "You remember what we've agreed on, right?"

"Of course. The two of us were never here. You came over with my dad to talk about the whole heir situation, and he and Faye's dad had a major disagreement which ended with the both of them dead and you injured but alive."

He nods. "Okay, so I guess the only thing left is for me to be *actually* injured to make sure the story is believable. Go ahead, Faye."

Faye pulls her fist back and, with carefully measured strength, punches Boss in the arm; there's a snapping sound as the bone breaks, and she winces. "Sorry."

"It'll heal," Boss says, grimacing in pain, but he smiles at them. "Come on, you two. Make yourselves scarce."

"Thank you," Faye says, and she hugs him, carefully avoiding his arm.

Maddie hugs him in turn. "Thank you," she says. "We'll come visit."

"Call ahead if you do, we don't want anyone to see the three of us together," he replies. "But I'll be glad to see you. Now shoo."

Faye and Maddie both nod, they join hands and walk out of the mansion. Once they've put some distance between them and the building they pause.

The sun breaks over the horizon as they kiss.

"So, where do you want to go?" Faye asks.

"Wherever. It doesn't really matter," Maddie replies. "As long as I'm with you, any place is fine."

They kiss again and, hand in hand, start running, giggling as they go.

A Christmas Gift

I
I'll Be Home for Christmas

There's a soft knock at the door, then a voice asks, "Todd? Coz? Can I come in?"

Todd pauses the game and turns around. "Yeah, of course," he says. "Right now it's your room too, after all."

"Only while we're here," Alan says, stepping into the room. "I'm just going to grab the presents from my suitcase, and Steven's too. Oh, and your mom said to tell you to come downstairs for the gift exchange."

Todd sighs. "I'll be right down."

Todd sighs again as Alan leaves. It's useless. No matter how hard he tries, he can't manage to exchange more than a couple words at a time with his cousins. It's weird, actually, since they're all nearly the same age and their family is close-knit. And yet he's always had trouble relating to the boys, and ever since he started puberty, he's found himself keeping his distance from the girls — he finds talking to them to be more than a bit awkward.

Still, his mom keeps trying to push him to be sociable, especially now that Alan and Steven are sleeping on air mattresses in his room for a full week. It's the only space available, since Uncle Murray and Aunt Amy are in the guest room and their daughter Rachel is on the fold-out couch in the den.

Todd's parents had told him about the sleeping arrangements when he'd come home for Thanksgiving, and he'd almost decided not to come back home for Christmas at all. But when he'd broached the subject both his parents had frowned deeply. Todd, always the dutiful son, had quickly dropped the subject and made plans to be home for Christmas.

Ah well, at least this way he can spend some time with his grandma. They've always been very close, living in the same house and all, but she's getting on in years. She can be a bit forgetful nowadays and it's better to make the most of it while she's still mostly lucid. Better to make memories now rather than have regrets down the line.

A shout of "Todd!" from downstairs shakes him out of his reverie. He shakes his head and sighs deeply once again. *Better get down there or I'll never hear the end of it*, he thinks, and gets up. He carefully steps over the two air mattresses and makes his way downstairs, pausing briefly to put on the ugly Christmas sweater hanging behind the door, even though he hates the thing. The wool is all felted up and threadbare in places — Todd's worn the thing every Christmas since he was nine, when it was so big it hung like a tent over his body — and it's remarkably itchy. (How is it even *possible* for a sweater to be itchy through his shirt anyway? It's not like it makes contact with his skin.) He'd very much prefer not to wear it, but it's a family tradition. Everyone will be wearing one, and everyone will complain if he doesn't wear it, so wear it he does.

They're all waiting for him, and he feels them watching as he descends the staircase. He always hates being the center of attention. But he's brought this on himself, holing up in his room since lunch, so he just bears it. He also bears Uncle Murray bellowing, "There you are, boy! I was wondering if you'd show up at all!"

"Here I am," Todd replies, smiling awkwardly.

"You're late, son. Come on, we were waiting for you," his father says, pointing at a spot on the floor. Todd sits down as directed, cross-legged, next to Steven, who is sitting beside Rachel, who is trying to find a comfortable place on the floor between her brothers — it's not easy, because between Todd, Steven, Alan, Rachel, and their other cousins, Mike and Hannah, there's very little wiggle room. This, at least, makes Todd smile. Some things never change, like the kids being made to sit on the floor while the adults claim the sofas and armchairs even though the 'kids' are now all over twenty.

Jennifer, Todd's grandmother and the matriarch of the family, is, as always, sitting in the place of honor next to the fireplace in which a small fire is happily crackling away. She's nestled cozily into the recently-restored vintage armchair that used to be her mother's, and her mother's mother's before that, and which will be her daughter Mary's — Todd's mother's — after Jennifer eventually passes.

After Mary, the chair — and the title of matriarch along with it — will likely pass on to Rachel as the next-eldest woman in the family who's related to Jennifer by blood, since Mary has neither sisters nor daughters. Todd always feels a bit sad that he can't inherit the armchair himself, but he puts on a cheerful face and says, "Hi, Grandma," as he looks up at her.

"Hello, dear," she replies, smiling warmly at him. "Did you have fun playing with your video games?"

"I did," he says. "I spent the afternoon climbing a mountain."

She raises an eyebrow at him. "Oh? I didn't know you could climb mountains on your computer."

"Well, not *literally* climbing a mountain, but there's this game about a girl who decides to go climbing, just to prove she can."

"Oh, I get it," she considers pensively. "She climbs the mountain because it's there. As a personal challenge. Makes perfect sense, many people have done that before."

"Yes. And—"

"Why don't you tell her later, Todd?" His mother interjects. "We have to open the presents. It's already late, and Uncle Tony and Aunt Clare have quite a way to go before they get home, so they have to get going soon."

"Right." He nods. "Sorry. Go ahead."

The gift exchange is a quick affair. Everyone is grown up after all, they're all well past the point where they get excited by having to unwrap enormous boxes, along with huge numbers of smaller packets. Todd receives practical gifts, stuff he can use when he goes back to college after the holidays: a new notebook, a few pens, and a laptop case.

Then, to his surprise, Grandma Jennifer picks up the large box beside her armchair and hands it to him. "For me?" He asks, his eyebrows disappearing into his hairline.

"Yes, for you, dear." Jennifer smiles.

Todd looks at her for a moment, then takes the box from her. It's surprisingly light for its size and wrapped carefully in red and gold paper. He turns it over a few times, running his fingers over the surface to find the tape and carefully unstick it — his mother has taught him not to rip the paper when unwrapping gifts so that it can be reused. He folds the paper back, unsticks some more tape, and opens the fancy-looking cardboard box. Inside is a bunch of light pink, almost see-through tissue paper, and inside *that*...

He touches something that feels like cloth but then snaps his hand back as he feels a brief stinging pain. "What's the matter?" His father asks.

"Nothing," he says, shaking his head. "Just a static shock. Let's see now..."

Todd reaches into the box again, pulls back the pink paper, and freezes.

What?!

No, hold on.

...*What?!*

He blinks. No, it can't be. Grandma didn't really give him—

"What's the matter, Todd?" His mother says. "Show everyone what Grandma gave you."

Todd woodenly looks up at her. He gulps and awkwardly nods. Carefully he extracts the black lingerie set from the box, holding it up for everyone to see: bustier, thong panties, garter belt, and silky stockings — all on full display.

Seriously, *what the hell?*

He laughs nervously. "Uh...Thanks, Grandma, but...uh..."

"You're welcome, dear."

He doesn't know what to say, so he just gulps again.

It's his mother who fills the silence. "Oh, good thinking, Mom!" she exclaims. "Todd really needed a new pair of winter socks, all the ones he has are almost threadbare."

Todd blinks at her. "Winter socks?" he asks.

"Yeah, I can see from here. They're clearly *winter* socks. You know, wool, as opposed to cotton?"

A CHRISTMAS GIFT

"Or microfiber," Uncle Murray adds. "Those are good for the summer. They keep your feet dry, you know, but they're very light."

"Wool keeps your feet dry, too," Rachel interjects.

"Oh really?"

"Really. Many runners use wool socks. I do, too."

"Huh, didn't know that."

"But anyway, those look really nice," Mary says, pointing at the lingerie Todd is still holding up. He looks at it, and then at her.

"Are you sure these are winter socks?" he asks.

"They look like winter socks to me," she replies, and then turns to Jennifer. "Where did you get them, Mom?"

"I made them myself. They're special," Jennifer says, and she winks at Todd.

"Aw, that's a shame. I'd have liked to get a pair for myself. Anyway, they're very nice."

Todd finds himself nodding. "Yeah. Thanks, Grandma." *What is even happening?* he thinks, looking around the room, bewildered. Except for Mary, Jennifer, and Rachel, who've launched into a discussion about the merits of various types of yarn and fabric in handmade clothing, the conversation seems to have moved on. No one is paying attention to him or to the clearly-not-winter-socks *things* he's still holding up as if in a daze. Is he being pranked? Are they all in on it?

He shakes his head, dismissing the thought as soon as it comes to him. No. Even though he doesn't get along with most of them, nobody in his family is the type to play this kind of trick on him. But if he's not the victim of a practical joke, why is everyone convinced the lingerie is a pair of winter socks?

This is *weird*.

"Well, this was fun," Uncle Tony says, getting to his feet, "but unfortunately, we have to get going if we want to get home at a reasonable hour. Come on, kids."

Mike and Hannah pull themselves up from the floor, and start saying goodbye to their cousins, while Uncle Tony shakes the hands of his brothers-in-law, and Aunt Clare kisses both Mary and Aunt Amy on the cheek. "Thanks for having us," she says. "Lunch tomorrow?"

"Of course," Mary says with a smile.

And then they're gone. Todd's father and Uncle Murray move to the den for a late-afternoon drink, while Steven, Alan, and Rachel start talking among themselves. Todd turns to his mother. "Do you need a hand in the kitchen?"

"No, sweetie, I can manage. You can stay here and talk with your cousins."

Or go up to my room instead, he thinks as he heads for the stairs with his gifts. Grandma Jennifer intercepts him before he reaches the first step.

"I hope you liked my gift," she says, smiling warmly.

"It's lovely," Todd says. "But I don't—"

She stops him by pressing a finger to his lips. "You'll understand in time. Come talk to me when you do."

He looks at her for a few moments before nodding. "Goodnight, Grandma," he says.

"Goodnight, dear. Sleep well."

He hugs her and kisses her cheek, then climbs up to his room, where he dumps his presents on his desk. He's about to resume playing his game, but then hesitates, looking at the box.

Slowly, with uncertain hands, he opens it and pulls out the lingerie set again.

It *is* lovely. All black, most of it lace. It looks like it's his size, too. Maybe—

No.

No, don't go there, Todd, he tells himself firmly. He knows from experience that nothing good can come from trying it on. His body isn't even the right shape anyway.

Best to put it back in the box, slide the box under the bed, and forget all about it.

But somehow, he can't bring himself to do it. He stares at the flimsy underclothes for a long time and, in the end, the box does go under the bed, but the lingerie set he hangs behind his door, and he keeps sneaking peeks at it while he makes the girl on the screen leap over gaps and rush up slopes.

He's still thinking about it when he goes down to the pantry to grab a cereal bar for dinner, and he's still thinking about it when he goes to bed and falls asleep.

II
Baby It's Cold Outside

A FAMILIAR TUNE, playing faintly, draws Todd from the depths of sleep. He frowns slightly before opening his eyes, since he can also hear his cousins, talking in hushed tones, occasionally swearing. What are they doing?

"Mmm..." he mumbles, turning over in bed to face the source of the noise. He opens his eyes, stretches, and yawns.

"Oh, damn, sorry, were we too loud?" Steven asks, looking up from the game console Alan is holding. "We should've been quieter. Our bad." Alan, for his part, just nods, face screwed in concentration as he taps on the controls.

Todd shakes his head. "No, you weren't being too loud." He glances out of the window and sees it's already light. "It's way past the time I usually wake up anyway, so don't worry about it." He stretches again. "What are you doing?"

"Trying to get past this effin' screen, that's what we're doing," Alan says. A noise comes from the console and he sighs. He pauses the game. "And that's five deaths. Your turn, Bro."

Steven grabs the console and unpauses it, moves the lever of the joypad, and swears. "Okay, that one didn't count." Then he quirks his mouth in thought. "You know, why don't you try?" he asks, looking up at Todd.

"What? Me?" Todd asks, blinking.

"Yeah, this is your specialty after all. Just get us past this screen, and we'll manage."

Todd looks at his cousins, who are watching him expectantly, then he pulls himself out of the covers and sits on the edge of the bed. "Give it here," he says, beckoning.

Alan and Steven join Todd on the bed, handing him the console. He looks down at the familiar game. "Oh, yeah, I see, this is a tricky screen. It's designed so it plays with your head, it makes you pick the wrong path."

"Oh, so we're not supposed to be going up and over?" Alan asks, pointing.

"No, you're not. Or at least not yet," Todd replies, shaking his head. "Not at your skill level."

"Hey!" Steven laughs, lightly punching Todd in the shoulder. "I'll have you know we're quite skilled at this game!"

"Not enough, sorry," Todd replies, laughing along. "This path is faster, but you need to be very precise with your inputs, almost frame-perfect, so you don't usually go for it outside of a speedrun. Instead, you should go down, double jump to clear the spike block, and then dash up and right to reach the other side of the gap." He demonstrates. "See? It's longer, but easier."

"Huh, cool. Thanks, Coz."

"You're welcome. That'll be ten dollars, please."

"We'll buy you coffee the next time we're in town," Alan says.

"Deal." Todd checks his watch. "Wow, is it already that late? We should make ourselves presentable, Aunt Clare and Uncle Tony'll be here soon."

"Yeah, can't greet them in our PJs. Mind if I take the bathroom first?" Steven asks.

Todd nods, and Alan says, "Go ahead," before starting to root inside his suitcase. When Steven returns a few minutes later, Alan's frowning.

"What's the matter?" Todd asks.

"Forgot my shaving kit," Alan replies. "I didn't notice it yesterday because I shave every other day. Can I borrow your razor?"

"Why are you asking him?" Steven says. "You know he doesn't shave. He doesn't need to."

I don't? Todd thinks, frowning slightly. He touches his cheek and, indeed, it's smooth as a baby's bottom. But he remembers it being rough like sandpaper the previous evening. What's going on?

He shakes himself as Alan answers, "Well, he shaves his legs, doesn't he?"

"No, I epilate," Todd answers reflexively. "And the type of razor you use for your legs isn't good for your face in any case." His frowns deepens. *Why the hell did I say that?* He shakes his head to clear it. "Can't you borrow Steven's?"

Steven chuckles. "Sorry, haven't shaved in years," he says, running his fingers through his bushy beard. "I have the clippers I use to keep it tidy, but that's not what Alan needs."

"Yeah," Alan says, sighing. "Ah well, I'll just go out and buy a disposable razor. You two wanna come with?"

"Yeah, sure," Steven replies, and he pulls the curtains aside slightly. "We should cover up, though, I can see some ice on the ground."

They all change quickly, picking heavy clothes to ward off the cold. Todd takes the opportunity to briefly run his hands up and down his naked legs: smooth, just like his face. Weird. He pulls on a sweater — not the ugly Christmas one. "Ready."

"What, you're not going to put those on?" Alan asks, jerking his thumb toward the lingerie set, still hanging behind the door.

Todd looks at it and then at him. "No," he says slowly, carefully. "Bit too fancy to put on just to go into town, don't you think?"

"Right. Best to save them for a special occasion," Steven says. "Why did you hang them behind your door anyway?"

"It felt a bit bad to just leave them in the box," Todd replies, still slowly and carefully. "I mean, Grandma went to the trouble of making them for me."

Steven glances at them again. "And they're very nice. They kinda complement the room's decor."

Alan laughs as he opens the door and starts down the hallway. "How does a pair of winter socks complement a room's decor?" he asks. "Seriously, bro."

"I don't know, but they do," Steven says. "They're nice."

Todd nods in agreement. "They *are* nice." Because they are.

"Oh, are you boys going somewhere?" Uncle Murray asks from the couch where he and Todd's dad are watching a game.

"Yeah, just for a walk in town," Todd replies. "We won't be long."

"See that you aren't," Todd's dad says. "You know your mom doesn't like when you're late for lunch."

"Oh, come on, Uncle Walt, lunch is just leftovers from yesterday anyway," Alan says.

"Still. Don't be late, boys."

"Yeah, yeah," Steven says with a laugh and a wave. "See ya later!"

The three of them grab their coats and venture out. Even though the sun is shining brightly, it's still a particularly chilly morning. Steven was right, it must be well below freezing. The sidewalks are indeed a bit iced over, and they have to be careful not to slip as they walk down the hill. Todd briefly wonders how the other girls do it. He's already having a bit of trouble keeping his balance, and he's wearing boots. He can't even imagine what it would be like to make the trek in heels.

"You're taking part in the yearly speedrunning marathon in a couple weeks, right?" Alan asks.

"Yep. I was lucky I managed to get a spot," Todd replies. "The competition is really fierce."

"We knew you would make it, though," Steven interjects. "You're, like, the third fastest in the world, aren't you? And your streams are really fun."

"You watch my streams?"

"Of course. They're just the right balance of entertaining while also showing off technical skill. You probably never noticed us in the comments because you get what, five thousand viewers every time you stream?"

"I peaked at eight thousand during my last world record attempt."

"See? You're famous, Coz."

"Only Internet famous."

"Still famous," Alan says. "We'll be cheering you in the comments during the marathon."

"See that you don't embarrass me, please."

Steven puts on a mock-scandalized face. "Embarrass you? Perish the thought! We would never. Oh, there's the store," he adds, pointing, as they step into the town square.

Todd peers ahead. "Looks like it's closed, though."

The store is, indeed, closed, and as they take a look around they realize that *all the* stores are closed; after a moment of puzzlement they realize why.

"*Of course* the stores are closed," Alan says, groaning. "It's the day after Christmas. I should've realized most stores would be closed for the holidays. And you both came with me, too. Sorry."

"It's not a problem," Steven says, and Todd inclines his head in agreement.

"It's not like we had to trudge through the snow uphill both ways to get here," he jokes. "It was just a short walk. And it did us good to get out of the house and into some fresh air."

"I'm still sorry," Alan says. "Let me buy you coffee to make it up to you."

"So that's two coffees you owe me." Todd grins.

"I'll buy you a doppio and be done with it," Alan replies with a laugh.

They wander through the almost-deserted streets for a while and by some miracle they manage to find a small, hole-in-the-wall cafe that's open.

"We're in luck," Steven says, and he pulls the door open, motioning Todd inside. "Ladies first."

"Why, thank you," Todd replies with a smile, and he walks in, followed by his cousins.

As the door closes behind them, he stops dead in his tracks.

Wait, hold on, what the hell? he thinks. *Why am I being so friendly with Alan and Steven? And why did Steven say "Ladies First?!"*

He clearly remembers being on extremely awkward terms with them both, as well as the rest of his extended family. Just yesterday he'd exchanged all of two words with Alan, and none at all with Steven; he'd spoken with Alan mostly out of a sense of obligation — you have to talk with your cousins sometimes, right? Even if you don't like them all that much. And yet, now they're all behaving as if they're the best of friends and always have been.

This is *weird*.

"Todd? Coz? Everything okay?" Alan says from behind him.

Todd shakes his head, trying to clear it, and turns toward Alan and Steven. "Yeah, everything's fine. Let's find a table."

They sit down, order and keep chatting.

"Still don't know how you manage to balance streaming with college," Alan comments. "I can barely find time to study with my part-time job."

"Streaming doesn't take up that much time. I only do that three times a week for two hours, I have plenty of time for studying."

"Right. I wonder if I should just find something else, having to deal with moviegoers is just the worst. At least I get a few free tickets out of it."

"Oh, speaking of which," Steven says, "have you seen the latest *Mutant Vengeance*?"

"I have. It's terrible."

"It is, isn't it? The series really went to crap after the second one. Not like *Space Vindicators*, that one's still good."

"It's not, the last one was awful."

"Was not!"

"Was too."

As Alan and Steven start debating if, and when, superhero movies have jumped the shark and are just limping along out of inertia, Todd sips his latte — he decided against a doppio, that would be too much caffeine all at once — and smiles. Despite being bewildered by the whole thing, he's really enjoying the conversation; talking with his cousins is really nice. He briefly wonders why he didn't do it before or why he doesn't seem to be having trouble getting along with them now. He can't really relate to them, like he remembers, but that's fine too — after all, Steven and Alan are boys, and Todd is...

Todd is *what*? There's a thought there, just at the edge of his mind, but every time he tries to grab it, he finds it slipping away. He just can't seem to focus on it, for whatever reason.

But no matter. Whatever it is, it will come to him again in time. Or maybe not, and that will be fine too. For the time being, he's just enjoying talking with his family.

After they finish their coffees, they decide to head back home. Aunt Clare and Uncle Tony are probably already there. They keep chatting as they climb up the hill, too, and in short order they're back home. They're greeted by Mary and Jennifer at the door.

"Well, it took you long enough," Mary says, but she has a smile on her lips. "Come on, go wash your hands, I've almost finished warming the leftovers."

They quickly shed their coats, hanging them beside the door. Jennifer intercepts Todd before he can follow his cousins to the bathroom. "Good morning, dear, did you sleep well?" she asks.

"Yeah, I did," he replies. "Thanks, Grandma."

"That's good, that's good," she nods. "And what about this morning? Did you have fun with your cousins?"

"I did," he repeats.

"That's good, too," she says, and she winks at him. "Come on now, let's get to lunch."

Everyone is already seated at the table when they get there. Or at the *tables*, rather. There's no way they're all going to fit in the kitchen, so the table they usually eat at has been moved to the living room, and another table has been taken out of storage and pushed against it. This way, all thirteen of them can sit together, though it's tight.

Todd is surprised to realize that the place that's been left open for him is not his usual one, near the window and between his father and his uncle Tony, but is instead on the opposite end, right beside Hannah and Rachel — he'll be sitting on the women's side of the table. But then he shakes his head, not paying it any mind. What's a seat at the table anyway?

"So anyway, when we reached town, we realized that all the stores are closed," Todd says, ladling some stuffing on his plate before passing the bowl along.

"We could've told you that before you rushed out in the first place if you'd only thought to ask," his mom replies.

"Hey now, I was just going along with Steven and Alan, it was their idea."

"We could tell," Rachel comments. "It's just like them to not plan ahead. Typical boy mentality."

As a giggle runs along the people on their side of the table, Steven looks up from the conversation he's been having to loudly — and jokingly — protest, "Hey! Just because we're not there it doesn't mean you can badmouth us!"

"Yes we can!" Hannah calls back. "What are you gonna do about it?"

"Beat you at *Clue* later, that's what!"

"You're on!"

"See? Typical boys, always competitive," Aunt Clare says under her breath, making the gaggle of girls — and Todd — around her burst into giggles again.

It's weird, though: while he'd had no real trouble talking with his male cousins earlier, Todd has even less trouble talking with his female relatives. It's as if he has much more in common with them than he had with the boys. It's a strange feeling, but very nice in its strangeness, so he just puts the whole situation out of his mind.

After the plates are cleared away, his mom and dad break out the board games. There's some initial confusion as to how to form the teams, since there's seven women and six men at the table, but then Todd's grandmother excuses herself to go take her nap, evening out the numbers, so they divide themselves into four teams: the men, the boys, the women, and the girls — with Todd. There's something about how the people around the table were split that bothers him a bit, something he can't quite put his finger on. But then he dismisses it as a trick of his imagination and gets to playing.

It's really fun, especially because his team wins.

By the time they're done it's late, and he realizes that this is probably the first time he's ever felt completely at ease spending the whole day with his family. It's a nice feeling, and he wonders why he hasn't done it before.

As he gets ready for bed that night his eyes fall once again onto the lingerie set hanging behind his bedroom door.

Maybe...?

He shakes his head. No. It would probably fit him, but it would be awkward if his cousins came into the room unexpectedly and found her wearing it. I mean, they're still boys, and it would be weird for them to see their cousin in her underwear, right?

She finishes putting on her PJs, tucks herself into bed, and is fast asleep before she knows it.

III
Let It Snow

Todd wakes up as she feels a draft sneaking its way under the covers, chilling her. She mumbles, grabs the duvet, and tries to pull it over herself, but someone yanks it back from the other side, uncovering Todd completely.

She sighs in exasperation. Four nights of sleeping in the same bed, and Rachel is still hogging the covers. It's probably better if she uses one of her parent's larger duvets for the remaining nights, Todd decides. Maybe then she and Rachel won't have to play tug-of-war any longer.

She opens a bleary eye and takes in the room, lit by the dim rays filtering through the window. Judging by their color, the sky is probably cloudy, but it's still light enough to make out the air mattress on the floor next to the bed. It's probably best if they get up. They were planning on going shopping that morning and they're already burning sunlight.

She jabs a knuckle into Rachel, who's wrapped in the duvet like a silkworm in a cocoon. "Hey. Wake up," Todd says; Rachel mumbles, and turns over, dragging the covers along with her. Todd sighs and prods her. "Hey. Wake up, bitch."

"'m not a bitch, you're a bitch," Rachel replies sleepily.

"Neither of you is a bitch," says a voice from the air mattress. "You're both very loud, though. Very loud girls. And I was trying to sleep."

The final sentence is almost drowned by a yawn and goes right over Todd's head as a thought shoots through her mind: *Wait, what? I'm not a girl.*

She reaches down, pats her body, and pauses, perplexed; it definitely *feels* like a girl's, but... She can almost recall, at the edge of her consciousness, that it feels different somehow. It feels like she's not used to it.

She pulls herself up on the bed, frowning deeply. Rachel feels the movement and looks up at her. "Todd? What's wrong?" she asks.

"I...don't know," Todd replies. "I'm...I..."

Rachel matches her frown. "Girl, you alright?"

Todd looks at her. "Am I a girl? Rach, am I really a girl?"

Rachel blinks. But then, after a moment, she says, "Hey. Hey now, no, Todd, it's okay. Come on." She unspools herself from the covers and pulls herself up to a kneeling position, putting a hand on Todd's shoulder. "It's alright. Deep breaths."

"Mmm...What's happening?" The figure on the air mattress says, turning over, and Todd is startled to see that it's Hannah. But then she remembers — the previous day Hannah decided to sleep over, too, since they wanted to go shopping in the morning.

"I think Todd is having a bit of a dysphoria attack," Rachel says, not looking at Hannah. She's keeping her eyes fixed on Todd. "Todd? Hey. Come on, it's alright. I know it's hard to see yourself in the mirror sometimes, but you have to remember that you're a girl." She leans forward and embraces Todd, holding her tight. "And a really pretty girl, at that."

"Yeah, seriously," Hannah says, standing up and walking over to the bed. She places a hand on Todd's shoulder and continues, "Only an idiot would think you're a boy."

Todd looks at her and then at Rachel. After a moment, she smiles. "Yes, you're right. Thanks."

"You're welcome," Hannah says. "What brought this on, though? You seemed fine yesterday."

Rachel bites her lip. "Wait, Todd, when was the last time you injected?"

Todd thinks back. "I...don't know? I can't remember."

"Figures," Rachel says and sighs. "Todd, you *know* you have to get your HRT at regular intervals. Otherwise, you get emotional and dysphoric. Come on, let's get you stabbed."

She reaches over and pulls open the drawer on Todd's nightstand. She extracts several items from it: a single-use syringe, wrapped in plastic; an ampule of some kind of liquid; a bottle of rubbing alcohol; and a cotton swab. Todd frowns. What are those doing in there? She's sure she's never seen them before.

"Pull up your shirt," Rachel says, and Todd instinctively complies. "Hannah, take this. Warm it up, it'll flow better." She hands Hannah the ampule, then dabs some alcohol on the cotton pad and disinfects Todd's abdomen, off to the side of her belly button.

"Cold," Todd complains.

Rachel grins at her. "Don't worry, we're almost done."

She wordlessly holds her hand out toward Hannah, who hands her the ampule. She disinfects the rubber stopper, too, and then draws some liquid from the tiny vial with the syringe. Then, pinching Todd's skin, she sticks her with the needle and slowly injects the hormones.

"All done," Rachel says, replacing the plastic cap on the syringe's needle and smiling at Todd.

"Thanks, Rach," Todd replies, massaging the spot like she's been taught to do, to help absorption.

"You're welcome," her cousin replies. "But you should really learn how to do injections yourself, I can't always be here to help you." She frowns. "Wait, how *did* you get your E into you while you were at college?"

"I asked my roommate. She's studying nursing, so she knows how to do it," Todd replies. And then she frowns in turn. *Did I really do that? I can't remember*, she thinks.

"Yeah, that makes sense," Hannah says, shaking Todd out of her thoughts. "But Rach is right, you really should learn to do it yourself." She pauses. "You alright? Dysphoria's all gone?"

Todd takes a moment to take stock of her feelings and then nods. "Yeah, for the moment at least. Sorry for worrying you, you two."

"Don't even think about it," Hannah replies, dismissing the apology with a wave of her hand. "I know you can't control it — no harm done. I'm glad you're okay."

Rachel nods in agreement. "And you know what we can do to make sure dysphoria doesn't come back?" she asks.

Todd inclines her head to the side. "Shopping trip?"

"Shopping trip!" Rachel confirms. "Come on, get dressed. We have Christmas money to spend."

As Rachel and Hannah get dressed, Todd walks to the bathroom and washes her face, thankful once more that she doesn't need to shave any longer — the laser and electrolysis took care of that. Her last session was a couple months before. She takes the time to carefully apply some make-up, just a bit of eyeliner and some lipstick. She's been told she doesn't really need it, that she looks good regardless, but she's not confident enough in her looks to leave the house without putting some on. *And besides, it's fun,* she thinks, painting her lips a pale shade of pink and smiling at herself in the mirror.

"You done in there?" Hannah calls, knocking on the door. "I have to pee."

"Go ahead," Todd replies, opening the door and stepping back into the bedroom. As Hannah closes the door, Todd hesitates and looks at Rachel. "Uh…Do you mind if I change in here?" she asks.

"Why would I mind?" Rachel says. "We're all girls here, after all."

Todd nods and smiles at her. "Thanks, Rach."

"Any time, Coz."

Quickly shedding her PJs, Todd stops for a moment, frowning down at her penis. It's smaller than she remembers. But hormones will do that, won't they? And the changes have been coming more and more quickly lately. Take her breasts, for example: while not large by any stretch of the imagination, they're already big enough to fill an A cup, though barely.

She glances at the black, lacy lingerie set, hanging behind the door, briefly considering whether to put that on. No, better not — it's way too fancy for just a day out in town. She grabs a simple cotton bra instead, asking Rachel for her help to fasten it — "Seriously, Todd, you'll have to learn to do it yourself sooner or later," Rachel chides her — and matching cotton panties. Then pantyhose, a wide skirt (to help hide *it*, so she doesn't have to tuck as tightly), a nice top, and a cute sweater.

She turns to look at herself in the mirror, strikes a pose, and smiles.

"Yep, you look cute," Rachel says. Hannah sticks her head out of the bathroom, bobbing her head up and down in agreement. "And, if you get dysphoric again, remember, we think you're a beautiful girl, so you should listen to us instead of your dumb brain."

"Thanks, Rach," Todd says. "Thanks, Han."

"You're welcome," Hannah replies. "Shall we be off?"

Todd nods, and they move downstairs. "Oh, good morning, girls!" Todd's mom shouts from the kitchen. "Breakfast?"

"No, thank you, Aunt Mary," Hannah calls back. "We'll grab something in town."

"Okay! Wear sensible shoes, it's icy outside!"

"Okay!"

As they leave the house, Todd looks up at the dark gray clouds, which look just about ready to release their snowy load onto the town.

"Let's go, girls," she says, lengthening her pace. "We better hurry, or— Whoa!" she exclaims as her foot slips.

"Careful!" Hannah says, reaching out and grabbing Todd's arm.

Todd takes a moment to regain her footing then nods. "Thanks, Coz."

"You're welcome. But you really should've listened to Aunt Mary," Hannah replies.

"Yeah," Rachel pauses and points at Todd's heeled boots. "Those don't look like sensible shoes to me."

"Hey, come on, it's barely a one-inch heel," Todd laughs.

"Looks more like two inches to me."

"Whatever. Let's go, we want to get back before it starts snowing."

≣

"I'm telling you, you should've bought that top," Rachel says.

"Yeah, probably, but it showed a bit too much skin for my tastes," Todd replies. "And also…"

"And also…?" Hannah prompts, when Todd doesn't continue.

Todd bites her lip. "It makes my shoulders look big."

Rachel smiles kindly at her. "How many times do we have to tell you, Todd? Your shoulders are fine."

"They don't feel fine," she mumbles under her breath.

"But they are. I know you're worried, but you look no different than me or Han. You look more feminine than us, actually."

"Seriously," Hannah interjects. "I don't think you've bought a single pair of pants today."

"I like skirts better," Todd protests. "Sue me."

"No suing here, you look great in them."

"And you looked great in that top, too," Rachel adds.

"...Thanks."

"But thinking about it, it's good that you didn't buy it. How are we even going to carry all of that back to the house?" Hannah asks, pointing at the mountain of shopping bags next to their table. "Especially since it's snowing. Seriously, girls, you bought way too much."

"Yeah, probably," Todd replies. "But it's not our fault that they had lots of nice stuff."

"And, you know what they say when you can't pick between two things?" Rachel adds. "Both."

"Both," Todd says.

"Both," Rachel repeats.

"Both is good," they say in unison.

Hannah sighs. "You two are hopeless."

"Oh, come on, you had fun, too," Rachel says, elbowing her, and Hannah smiles.

"Rachel? Rachel Conley?" A man about their age is walking toward them. "Is that you?" he says.

"Warren!" Rachel exclaims, rising to her feet. "Dude! How are you?"

She embraces him, and Warren laughs. "You bitch, how long have you been in town? You could've told me you were back," he says.

"I'm just home for the holidays, barely a week," Rachel says. "You know how it is."

"Yeah, yeah," Warren says, stepping back from the hug. "So, you gonna introduce me?"

"Of course. Girls, this is Warren, we went to high school together."

"We also dated for a few months, but we made a terrible couple."

Rachel nods. "We broke it off mutually. Better to remain friends than try too hard and ruin everything. Warren, these are my cousins, Hannah and Caitlin."

"Hi," Hannah says. Cait waves.

Warren inclines his head to the side. "Hannah I remember seeing around once or twice, but did you have another girl cousin? I thought you had just the one."

Rachel gives him a wary look. "No, I have two."

"Huh, weird. I must be misremembering. It's strange, because I would usually remember such a cute girl." He smiles at Cait.

Cait smiles back nervously. Leaning heavily on all the voice training she's done — voice high and bright, forward in her mouth, feminine and friendly — she says, "Thank you for the compliment."

"You're welcome. Sorry, gotta dash now, I'm here with family," Warren replies, and he jabs a thumb over his shoulder at a table on the opposite side of the cafe. "But, Rach, listen, we're having a New Year's party on the thirty-first. Do you wanna come? You two, too, if you want," he adds, looking at Caitlin and Hannah.

"Yeah, of course. Sounds fun," Rachel replies.

"See you then," Warren says, and he walks off.

Rachel looks at him go for a moment, then she sighs and sits back down at the table. "Phew. That went well. Not that I think Warren would've had any problem with... But best to be safe."

"Thanks for the cover," Caitlin says. "You really saved me."

"No," Rachel says, shaking her head. "You saved yourself. See, what did I tell you? You *are* a cute girl."

Cait blushes and smiles at Rachel. "Thank you."

"You're welcome. So, you girls all done with your drinks? Good, then I'll call a rideshare, so we can get all of this stuff back home."

IV
That Spirit of Christmas

IT'S BEEN A while since Cait has had some time to herself, with all her cousins and aunts and uncles visiting. Not that she minds hanging out with them. They're the best family she could wish for, and she knows she'll miss them when the holidays are over. But sometimes, a girl needs some alone time, just to relax and to unwind.

And to try on the lingerie her grandmother gave her as a present for Christmas.

The bustier goes on first. She threads her arms into the straps, and then, with a well-practiced move, she fastens the thing behind her back, bending forward and placing her breasts into the cups with a swoop of her hands. It fits perfectly.

Then it's time for the stockings, which slide effortlessly up her smooth legs, and get clipped to the garter belt.

The panties are last — "Always put the panties on top of everything, or else you'll have to undo lots of stuff when you need to go pee," she remembers her girlfriends telling her — and they nestle nicely into position as she tucks her penis back between her legs.

And then she turns toward her tall mirror, fluffs back her shoulder-length hair, strikes a pose, and smiles, because she looks very good. No, more than good. She looks *hot*.

But after a moment she frowns, because she's remembered something — getting dressed up has unlocked a memory she'd forgotten. No, not *forgotten*. She's startled to realize that it was, somehow, sealed away.

And with that realization comes another one: there's someone she has to talk to. So, she puts on a robe, crosses the hallway, and knocks.

"Come in," says a voice from inside.

"Hi, Grandma," she says, closing the door behind herself.

"Hello, dear," Grandma Jennifer replies and then points at Cait's stockinged feet, visible below the hem of her robe. "I see you've put your present on."

"I did. It's nice."

"Glad to hear you like it. And those winter socks fit you perfectly."

Cait quirks her mouth. "They're not winter socks, Grandma, and you *know* that."

Jennifer chuckles softly. "Yeah. I do."

"Did you do this?" Cait asks accusingly. "Did you turn me into a girl? Because I've been thinking about it, and even though it seems incredibly far-fetched, it's the only explanation I can think of. Did you do it?"

"I did."

"Okay. How, exactly?"

"You see, dear, I happen to be the latest in a long line of...gift-givers, for lack of a better word," Jennifer explains. "In our family, we have a duty, passed down through the ages, to find people who are in need of help, and provide it. We untangle the lines of destiny, or tangle them as the need may arise, to allow people to live their best lives."

"And you do this by...magic, I assume." Jennifer nods, and Caitlin asks, "Are you a witch?"

"Not exactly a witch, but something like that," Jennifer says. "Some of our ancestors were persecuted as such, though. And, regarding the how, your case was simple. I just shunted us all onto a different timeline, one where you realized who you truly are at a relatively young age and started transitioning."

Caitlin frowns. "You should've asked permission," she says. "Not that I dislike this, mind you. I like who I am now, and I wouldn't have you undo it." She pauses. Quirks her mouth. "Could you undo it if I asked you to?"

Jennifer nods yet again. "Yes, I could."

"Okay. That's one point in your favor. But still, you should've told me what you wanted to do and asked for my permission to do it."

"Ah, but would you have given that permission? Would *Todd* have given that permission? Admitted who she really was and asked me to change her into a girl?"

It's a long time before Cait replies, and when she does, it's preceded by a sigh. "No," she says. "No, she wouldn't have. She'd have...refused."

"And you would still be Todd."

Caitlin silently nods.

"See, this is why I made it so you would remember," Jennifer says. "I could just as easily have had you forget about everything. About your previous life. But it's important to confront our pasts. To remember who we were. Don't you agree?"

"I do."

"I'm glad. And also, there's one more thing," Jennifer continues. "I told you about how I'm the latest of my line, right? Well, the gift-givers, the ones who carry on our duty, have all been women. *Are* all women. I was chosen by my predecessor when I was about your age. She taught and trained me, told me how to use our family's magic. And like her, I have to choose a successor, and teach and train her in turn."

"And whom did you choose?" Caitlin asks.

Jennifer doesn't reply. She just looks at her granddaughter, giving her a significant, capital-L Look. And Caitlin understands.

But she shakes her head.

"No. I'm sorry, Grandma, but no. I don't think I can do it."

Jennifer inclines her head to the side. "Why not?"

"Because...*Because*. You see, I understand who I am now. And I'm grateful for what you've done. I'm still a bit mad at you, but I'm also grateful. But when it comes to being your successor... Wouldn't it be better to pick Mom or Rachel? Or Hannah? You know, a..." She gulps. "A real woman."

"You stop with that talk right now, young lady," Jennifer says, leveling a finger at her. "You're as much a woman as your mom or your cousins. Or me, for that matter."

Caitlin shakes her head. "Thank you for saying that, Grandma, but you know I'm only like...like this," she motions down at herself, "because of the magic."

"And so am I."

It takes a few moments for Cait to fully register what her grandmother has just said. But after that, she stares at her, mouth agape. "...Come again?" she manages to stammer out after a few false starts.

"I said 'so am I,' Caitlin," Jennifer replies, smiling patiently. "Think about what those words mean. You'll get it."

"You're..." Cait begins. Then she shakes her head. It's just *not possible*. But Grandma Jennifer is looking at her expectantly, so slowly, carefully, Cait says, "You're *like me?*"

"I am. It was my aunt Darcie who passed the duty on to me. She saw something in me and gently broached the subject, and, well..." She smiles, and shrugs.

Caitlin looks at her for a long time, thinking about the revelation; then she asks, "So, where does Mom come from? I mean, if you're like me..."

Jennifer laughs. "Fair question. She comes from me. I chose to transform myself completely. Gave myself a womb, ovaries, the whole lot."

"You can *do* that?" Cait says, blinking in surprise.

"Sure can. You can do it too if you want, once I've taught you. Or you can choose to stay as you are. Keep your...keep *it*. You'll be a real woman regardless." She quirks her mouth. "Going back, I don't know if I'd make the same choice. I almost felt I had to, you know? I felt I wouldn't...be a real woman if I didn't complete the transformation. You and I are alike in that sense, too. And also, times were different. The world was less kind to people like you and me. But I got three kids and six grandkids out of the deal, so it wasn't all that bad, after all," she concludes with a smile.

"Were all those who came before us trans women?"

"Not all of them, but many. More than half, actually, I think? I'd have to check in the records."

"And how far back do the records go?"

"Since the beginning. Since Nikóla of Myra. She was the first one."

Caitlin inclines her head to the side and looks at Jennifer thoughtfully. "You said her name like I should know it, but I've never heard of her."

"I'm sure you have, but not by that name. She's quite well known, she's part of the history of Christianity, but unfortunately the Church decided to... What is that word you kids use these days? Deadname?" Caitlin nods, and Jennifer continues, "The Church deadnamed her in death, so everyone thinks she was a man. We, as her descendants and successors, are the only ones who know otherwise."

"Oh, that's a shame," Caitlin says, clicking her tongue. "Which Church was she part of?"

"There wasn't any real distinction back then. She was a saint, even."

Caitlin pauses. "No, wait, hold on."

Jennifer smiles. "Yes?"

"Saint... Nikóla, right?" Jennifer nods, and Cait continues, "And she was deadnamed in death, so assuming she used a similar name, that would make her..." She blinks. "No."

"Yes." Jennifer raises her brows.

"We're descended from fucking *Santa Claus?!*"

"Language, dear," Jennifer says, her smile turning into a smirk. "But I have to admit I said pretty much the same thing when my aunt told me about it back in the day."

Caitlin looks at her, mouth agape and then shakes her head. "Now I understand what you meant by 'a long line of gift-givers.' Holy shit."

"Yeah. Turns out, Santa is real and she's your grandma," Jennifer laughs. "But, going back to the point, what do you say about my proposal? I'd love to have you as an apprentice, my dear."

Cait sighs and bites her lip. "Let me think about it."

"That's all the answer I need right now. There's no rush, take your time." Cait nods pensively, and Jennifer continues, "So, what are you going to wear tonight?"

"For the New Year's party, you mean?" Caitlin asks, and when Jennifer inclines her head yes, she continues, "I don't know. I'm sure there's something in my closet that fits, but I still don't know what I'm going to pick."

"I have something for you, actually," Jennifer says, and she grabs a box off the floor and holds it out toward Caitlin, who looks at it and then up at her, frowning. Jennifer laughs again. "No, don't worry, this one is normal. Nothing magical about it, I swear."

Caitlin grabs the box and opens it. Inside is a black dress — a *short* black dress. It looks like it will barely cover her butt. It's form-fitting and will probably show a lot of cleavage, too. "This is a bit daring, don't you think?" She asks, holding it out at arm's length.

"It is. You don't have to wear it if you don't want to, of course, but I think it will help you make an impression. The boys will be all over you." Jennifer pauses, smiles mildly, and adds, "Or the girls. Or both. Or neither, that's fine, too. Also, it matches up nicely with my own dress."

"What are you going to wear?" Caitlin asks, and Jennifer holds up a deep red piece, which looks impressive and which Cait is sure will look incredible on her grandma.

"When you're at a party, you have to *party*," Jennifer says. "Why do you think I've been taking so many naps over the holidays? Gotta save up my strength. I want to keep going until two AM, at the very least."

Cait smiles. She clearly doesn't need to decide on whether to take her grandma up on her offer just yet — from how Jennifer is behaving, she has many years still in front of her.

Epilogue:
It's the Most Wonderful Time of the Year

The count-down reaches zero and everyone shouts "Happy New Year!" before taking a sip from their glasses. Caitlin smiles when she sees the red imprint her lipstick leaves on the crystal.

"Happy New Year, Cait," Rachel says, embracing her. Cait reciprocates the hug, and then, after disentangling, she hugs Hannah, too. Then her male cousins and a couple of strangers, too.

A CHRISTMAS GIFT

And then she spots Grandma, shaking her body on the dance floor. Even at her age, she's still got it. "Happy New Year, dear," Jennifer says when Caitlin approaches her. They clink their glasses and then exchange a hug. "How are you doing? Have you picked out someone to take home tonight yet?"

Caitlin laughs. "Come on, Grandma. I've been a girl for all of five days, it's still too soon for me to be thinking about...*that*."

"Right, right, sorry," Jennifer replies. After a moment, she adds, "What about Valentine's Day? I can introduce you to some people. My friends have plenty of grandkids of either gender. Of *all* genders, rather."

"*Grandma.*"

"Right," Jennifer laughs. "I promise I won't be too pushy." She pauses. "How are you holding up, Cait? Are you happy?"

Caitlin nods. "Yes. I'm happy. You still should've asked for my permission," she says, leveling a finger at her grandmother, "but I'm happy."

Jennifer nods back. "Good. That's good. Happy New Year Caitlin."

"Thanks, Grandma."

Afterword

When I first started writing, I did not quite expect the words I put on the page to resonate so much with people. I expected to write a handful of short stories and stop. Above all, I didn't expect to make money out of it.

But here I am, several books later, still chugging along, tapping on my keyboard, putting words out for people to read. Clearly I must be doing something right. Let's hope this continues.

Meanwhile, I have some people to thank, without whom I wouldn't still be here, in more ways than one. So let's get to it.

Thank you to Kate for deciding to take a chance on publishing this book and for putting in entirely more effort than strictly required to make it look as nice as it does. (Seriously: Antithesis Press is a small, up-and-coming publisher, but their quality is on par with, if not above, much bigger and well-established publishers. Please check out their catalog, there's lots of good stuff in there!). And to my sister Laura for once again providing the beautiful cover. (She's available if you need some graphic design done, wink wink nudge nudge.)

I would also like to thank the artist who goes by the handle GrumpyTG on various socials: one of their pieces was the spark of inspiration from which, with their permission, I adapted *A Christmas Gift*. (If you do decide to seek out their work, be aware that it's often explicit.)

Thank you to my family, for spurring me along in this little hobby of mine. And to my friends for constantly enabling my most terrible ideas.

Thank you to all my readers and to my patrons for their constant support and for their patience through my delays.

And thank you all for deciding to pick up this book and give it a read. Escaping inside the pages is too often one of the few distractions we have, so I hope you've enjoyed it.

Merry Christmas, everyone.

ABOUT THE AUTHOR

After decades of dreaming up and narrating stories for herself and for her family and friends, Zoe decided to turn pro and share her tales of the world as a way to distract herself from her day job and other assorted bleakness. When she's not writing she lives somewhere in Europe with two humans, a cat, and a turtle.

NTITHESIS PRESS is a small, radical press dedicated to amplifying Trans and Queer voices, preserving our histories, and challenging systems of oppression through storytelling. We believe in the transformative power of narrative to combat erasure, foster solidarity, and celebrate the vibrant diversity of trans and queer experiences. We believe that it is vital that our stories are shared and in doing so, preserved.

We publish Queer and Trans voices for Trans and Queer audiences, not books designed to apologetically make us palatable for cis-het audiences.

Through books, archives, and community collaboration, we strive to ensure that Trans and Queer stories are not only heard but remembered — because our histories are sacred, our voices essential, and our futures worth fighting for.

Patreon Supporters

Jade Allen
Erin Banneret
Alice Davis
Diana Green
Penelope Moore

www.ingramcontent.com/pod-product-compliance
Ingram Content Group UK Ltd.
Pitfield, Milton Keynes, MK11 3LW, UK
UKHW040238250426
12048UKWH00043B/1571